the BOY who FLEW

FLEUR HITCHCOCK

nosy crow

For Rosa, Ru and Ian, who have lived every second of this book's journey.

First published in the UK in 2019 by Nosy Crow Ltd
The Crow's Nest, 14 Baden Place
Crosby Row, London, SE1 1YW

Nosy Crow and associated logos are trademarks and/or registered
trademarks of Nosy Crow Ltd

Text © Fleur Hitchcock, 2019
Cover and chapterhead illustration © Ben Mantle, 2019

The right of Fleur Hitchcock to be identified as the author of this work
has been asserted by her in accordance with the Copyright, Designs
and Patents Act, 1988

Printed and bound in Great Britain by Clays Ltd, Elcograf S.p.A.
Typeset by Tiger Media

Papers used by Nosy Crow are made from wood grown in sustainable forests.

ISBN: 978 1 78800 438 1

www.nosycrow.com

Prologue

This could have happened. Or it could be happening now, somewhere, in a parallel universe.

Imagine yourself circling over a city.
A new golden, sharp-cut city, rising boldly towards the sky from its grubby roots. It teems with people and lights and rats and life and death.
It swarms, it breathes. It grows and shrinks.

But not all of the city is new.
To one side, an older shabbier cluster of houses teeters on the edge of the excitement.

Focus on one slender house. A jade dragon coils
around the candlestick, a red-shaded lamp glows in the drawing
room, but a bright light shines in the cellar.
Look again. Swing around until you're over the yard and you
can see inside.

It's not all dark; there are lanterns inside the kitchen.
Train your spyglass in through the tiny window panes.
There you'll find me.

ATHAN WILDE

Chapter 1

BANG!

The pomegranate becomes a red starburst and juice flows down the wall, crawling over the lumps in the plaster before pooling on the flagstones at my feet.

"Ha!" says Mr Chen at my side. "Ha!" And he dances a little jig.

"That," I say, picking up a small disc from the floor and licking the juice from my fingers, "was magic, total magic! Best one ever."

Bong!

Bong!

Bong!

Bong!

The clock on the church at the end of the row begins to strike midnight, the bell tolls, shaking through the walls of the old house.

Getting his breath back, and suddenly serious, Mr Chen leans forward and inspects the engine that fired the disc into the heart of the pomegranate. "Not magic, Athan boy, not magic. Not hocus-pocus or some god-fearing fairy dust. It was man that did it. *We* did it." He taps his sleek white hair. "With our clever heads."

"Yours more than mine," I say, taking a cloth and mopping the juice from the stones. "You're a genius, Mr Chen."

Moving silently alongside me Mr Chen closes his soft hand gently around mine. "No, Athan boy, I'm not, and I couldn't do it without you. Without your ideas. Your skill. You're as good as I am, in your way." He squeezes my arm. "Look how far we've come this past half a year." He swings around, touching on the mechanisms we've built. The small ones and the large ones, the apple picker and the rat trap, the parasol and the carrot slicer, the lamps, the pumps and finally the engine itself. "Look at it all and have more faith in yourself."

He coughs delicately into his handkerchief. "Now,

before I send you home, I want to try something else. We can't do this tomorrow. Tomorrow is Sunday, and you know how your mother and the God-fearers feel about Sunday. But tonight is still Saturday. Go and get the electric box down. It's heavy and I can't do it on my own."

"Really?" I say, blinking away tiredness and feeling suddenly awake. "Are we going to try out the bird?"

"Not yet." Mr Chen smiles, his eyes disappearing into the creases of his face. "We'll try her another day. Early one morning, when the days begin to lengthen."

"Oh." I wipe the juice from my fingers on to my breeches and duck into the little passage that opens from the kitchen into the store. I'm trying to hide my disappointment. I know it's the middle of the night but I had hoped.

I find a gap in the heavy velvet curtain and push through it to the heady smells on the other side.

Sulphur and ginger.

Oranges and vinegar.

Cinnamon and tar.

I love it in here. In another house it would be an ordinary larder, but nothing about Mr Chen is ordinary. Yes, there are nutmegs and cloves, pears and hams, but between the familiar packages there are strange brightly coloured bottles and boxes. Some marked with a skull and crossbones, others labelled with careful recipes.

While I'm pulling out a stool to stand on, he potters in behind me, humming and shuffling bottles around the shelves. Cobwebs catch in my hair as I climb but I reach out to the electric box sitting on the top shelf. It lurks blackly between a clear jar of vitriol and a box of raisins. It's heavier than it looks and I have to slide it down my chin and chest to keep it steady and even then I can feel the liquid slopping inside.

A large spider walks from the box on to my arm and then off my elbow to the next shelf down. I daren't brush it off; the box is too heavy.

"Here," I say, passing the box to Mr Chen, watching his old fingers stretch downwards with the weight.

"Excellent, excellent," he says, staggering from the store into the kitchen and thumping the box down on the table and lifting up the lid.

A sharp smell sneaks out and catches my throat, but the old man doesn't seem to notice as he adds a clear liquid from a stoppered bottle. "We're nearly ready to launch the bird, Athan, but where she is, we need a gale, and that gale must be from the north." He stares into space. "Or perhaps we can come up with another way to make her move fast enough. That can be your task, Athan." He beams at me. "Invent a launching machine for our bird."

"Wheels? A horse?" I suggest, taking the bottle from him. "Or we could lug her up to Lansdown, point her downhill, get her off the ground like a kite. If we could run fast enough, you know, trailing her behind."

Mr Chen laughs. "Perhaps." He clears his throat. "Ideas worth consideration, my boy, but they depend on who or what is watching." He fixes his gaze on mine. "We must take care of our bird. You have to understand that our flying machine could change the lives of thousands of people. Not all for the good." He fiddles with the plates of metal inside the electric box.

"How do you mean? Surely flying would always be a good thing?"

"How," he says, rearranging the insides of the electric box with a long pair of tweezers, "would you feel if your enemy came from the skies?"

"Like a seagull when it pinches your dinner?"

"Yes," he laughs. "Like a seagull dropping its bombs, but with bombs made of tar and brimstone – setting fire to the rooftops. How would that be?"

"But we can keep our bird for good people, so that it could do good."

"Exactly. And that's why we must be careful who

knows about it."

I listen to the strange tune Mr Chen hums and I try to retain what he's doing. Ever since he arrived like a kingfisher on a wet day last winter, with his boxes and bottles, colour and noise and laughter, I've been learning from him. No one's ever managed to teach me anything before, but Mr Chen's different. It's as if he knows everything – the why of everything, the truth. He annoyed Grandma straight away by knowing more than she did, explaining things, demonstrating things, laughing at her superstitions.

She was furious. Crossed her arms and said he was a devil.

But the devil chose me. I climbed down from the rooftops right in front of him and he looked in my eyes and said, "You'll do. You're just what I need."

From then on, he's given me work and paid me well.

"Excellent," mutters Mr Chen, and claps his hands lightly together. "Now, Athan boy – let us try again."

"Can we try not to break anything of Ma's this time?"

He shakes his head, remembering Ma's fury last Tuesday when we destroyed the henhouse. I thought she was going to hit him, and she's twice his size. "She has a fine tongue on her," he laughs. "But nothing will go wrong this time, and if it does, we'll give her some bananas," he says. "Now, Athan, get me the big engine."

I rummage in a cupboard and drag out a cluster of brass tubes set into a structure of wheels. It's heavy, but not as heavy as it looks, as it's mostly hollow. I set it on the table and unscrew the glass jar that acts as a tank, filling it only a little from a tarred barrel of clear liquid before screwing it back on top.

"Bananas," says Mr Chen, bending a piece of wire, "are very special, just as science is special." He slots the wire carefully into the tubes. "Today, science is also loud. Here, stick these in your ears."

He hands me two scraps of wadding and we crouch behind the table.

And then he touches the wires together.

BANG

BANG

BANG

BANG

BANG

BANG

BANG

BANG

BANG

The engine keeps beating, banging and thudding and shaking with a mechanical pulse that makes my eyeballs hurt. Faster and faster and more and more evenly, it beats and purrs and then the explosions become so close, so small and regular that it turns into a hum.

"The fan!" He reaches for an elegant-shaped wooden blade and attempts to jam the stalk of it into a hole in the engine.

But the fan catches, rips itself from his hand and flies across the room, passing us and whirring out of the open window. It bounces once on the cobbles and disappears. I listen for the impact, pulling the wadding from my ears.

Crash!

Glass.

Our window.

Mr Chen peers short-sightedly through the sash at our shop opposite. Three panes on the large window on the front have shattered. Two dresses on mannequins stand open to the weather behind a glittering heap of glass.

"My precious bananas it is then," he says, handing me a basket of yellow fruit. "And perhaps your kind uncle will be good enough to mend the breakages and send me the bill."

"Goodnight, Mr Chen," I answer. "Thank you for these."

"Thank you for all your help." He swings a pouch up from his belt and slips his hand inside. "Here." He drops four gold coins into my hand.

"But you don't owe me that much," I say, watching the coins reflecting on the glass of his thick spectacles.

"Take it," he says. "Just in case." And suddenly looking very tired, he waves me away.

Chapter 2

My dreams are full of flight. Mr Chen sits behind me, guiding my hand as I steer the flying machine over the city. Bouncing from river to river, spying on the rooftops, ducking the seagulls. We loop and buck and glide, driving straight for the moon, my heart high above my head, my soul free, the old man laughing in my ear. And then I wake.

I lie staring out at the blank upstairs windows of the house opposite, still half in my dreams, until I hear my name called.

"Athan, I need to go down now! Athan! Please."

It takes a moment for me to work out where and

when I am, and when I do, I realise that it's Beatty shouting from upstairs. Barefoot and part-dressed, I climb to her room on the floor above. She sits bird-like on her bed, her red blanket pulled up over her skinny shoulders, her bright eyes watching me. A big smile spreads over her face as I enter and she reaches her arms towards me.

A fledgling stuck in her nest.

"Athan. Tell me, why's Ma so cross?"

"Is she?"

"She's been stamping about this morning. Steaming. And now she's red with cross." Beatty screws up her face. "No – worse, she's white with cross. And it ain't just because of the windows."

"Boiling mad?" I ask, my heart sinking.

Beatty nods. "So why else? Athan, tell me!"

Downstairs, the kitchen's lit by a small lantern and even though it's light outside I blink in the daytime darkness. "Chair, Athan," says Beatty, her tiny fingers curled into my collar. I carry her over, balance her and her blanket on the stool by the range, and hold my hands to the empty fire grate. Almost no heat. A pot of cold porridge sits on the top; it must be hours old.

I reach into the kindling basket.

Empty.

Beatty shivers and pulls her red blanket closer over her shoulders.

"Morning, Poll. Morning, Ma," I say. "Any bread?"

Polly, my other sister, shakes her head. She sits in the almost darkness, stitching. Our giant ma picks at some embroidery by the window.

"Do something about the range, Athan," Polly says. "I've dye to boil." She nods here head at Ma, widening her eyes and drawing her finger across her throat.

"She'll cut you into chops, Athan," hisses Beatty. "She looks crosser than ever I seen her. I spec she's sorry you didn't blow yourself up with the windows."

"Hush, Beatty," murmurs Polly.

"Well, I spec she is. Look at her, she's like she sat on a porcupine."

Beatty's right. Ma's mouth is pinched. The lantern on the table lights her face but the lines seem deeper, her skin rougher. She looks old, tired. Sad.

"Morning, Ma!" I say again, pretending all's fine.

She doesn't answer.

Still in silence you could snap, I duck down by the fire and rake out the ash. Through more silence I take the fire bucket into the yard and breathe in the winter air.

Ice and chickens.

The good thing about destroying the henhouse is

the firewood that it left. The less good thing is that I've been trying to rebuild it out of rubbish from the building sites and I'm not so good at it. The structure I've built is a tower, held up more by luck than skill, a pile of badly hammered port wine boxes. The hens haven't been let out, but they follow me around the yard as I pick up wood because there's nothing to keep them in. There's nothing to stop the foxes either, only a branch of blackthorn balanced along the top of the wall. It's spiky with long nasty thorns, and it would keep everything out if it would just stay there. Which it does for a second before tumbling off.

For a moment I watch the hens pecking around my toes, enjoying their freedom. They shake their wings and jab at tiny insects, brushing against my legs, fearless and free.

I love to see them roam, but they won't last long like this. I'll get Tod to give me a hand with the henhouse. He'll know how to build one. He's good at that sort of thing.

Back inside, I place a dry leaf on a small lump of ember. I blow on it and the smoke rises in a lazy spiral. Some splinters of henhouse and a piece of newspaper catch and burn for a second before falling apart, and I feed more wood into the heat.

"So first I'm woken by breaking glass sometime in

the Lord-knows-when hours of the night and I come downstairs and find the shop window broken and the smell of his burning oils," says Ma.

"Ah," I say, looking around for the basket of bananas.

"So I wait for you to come back. I know you can't get back through the shop door, so I imagine you might climb the wall and come in through the kitchen and I wait on the stairs."

"Oh?" I say.

"But you don't," she says. "And what do I see next?"

I wince. I really hope she didn't go outside.

"Opposite, I see two boys, shinning up the gutter of the chapel – one of them the spit of Athan Wilde."

"Did you?" I say. "How … extraordinary."

"Extraordinary?" says Ma. "Athan, I've told you before – you could be killed up there or, worse, left a cripple. As if we didn't have enough to look after, what with your grandmother and all her…" Ma waves her hands at the petticoats drying above the stove, "… problems, and Beatty's legs and all." She sighs.

She's quite right, Tod and I did go roof running, but I open my mouth to deny it all when Polly shakes her head and points to a brown paper parcel by the door. I jump up from the stove side and grab it.

"Take it to the house with Mary, the pretty girl,

where the Clays used to be: New King Street," hisses Polly.

"Athan, don't go – listen." Ma catches my elbow, but her voice softens. "Don't you understand, boy? Those roofs are tall. Plenty of men have died building those houses. You could fall any time." She draws a shaky breath.

"I'm sorry, Ma, but..." I hold the parcel up, as if it's urgent.

"Please, son, you're a fine upstanding boy – almost handsome – we can dress you up, turn you into something, you can work for the Quality, they're always needing footmen, carriage boys. You can even work on the sedan chairs, they earn a fortune and they wear a lovely uniform. Get a job with a wig, something I can be proud of," she pleads.

We've had this conversation a thousand times before.

"Ma, I don't need to be a footman. I work for Mr Chen, I do the things he does. I'm getting to understand the way the world works, what makes things do the things they do. It's an education AND I'm earning money. Look – he gave me—"

"Oh, Athan!" She's taking it especially personally this time and her cheeks blotch. "If you wanted an education you'd have learned to read and write like your sisters. But that old man across the road – there's no future working for him, it's not a proper job. And," she says, looking into the small candle in the lantern, "he's evil. Your grandmother's right – he's a devil. It's not right, all that stuff he says."

I stand in the doorway ready to leave. "He's not evil, he's interested in real life, Natural Philosophy – all the ideas of clever men. It's different. He's teaching me—"

Ma slams her palms on the table. "He's teaching you rubbish. He's teaching you to make pretty sparks and purple smoke. What kind of thing is that for a grown man?" Her voice drops and she leans forward, into the darkness where I can't make out the expression on her face. "And I know he's encouraging you to dance around on the rooftops. You won't get anywhere on a rooftop!"

"There's a good reason for that. We're—" I begin.

"You're what, angels? Birds? Fly, can you?" she snaps. "If God had intended you to fly you'd have been born with wings. Well, I'll tell you something, Athan boy, you haven't got wings and you won't ever have them. Even those hens you love so much have more chance of getting off the ground than you do."

"You should see what he's—" She opens her mouth to argue again so I change tack. "All right, I promise,"

I say, my fingers crossed behind my back. "I promise not to go on the roofs any more, I promise to stay in at night if I'm not wanted for work – how's that?"

Ma seems to double in size. "I don't care a whit for your promises, boy. You're always promising things. I'll ask your uncle about getting you work directly I see him."

"But I work for Mr Chen!" I pull the gold coins from my pocket. "See!"

"Not any more you don't, boy." A metal voice grates across the flagstones of the kitchen floor. Grandma totters around the corner from the stairs. She's dressed in black with her face powdered white. She spots me at the door. "Not any more."

"What?" I say.

There's a long horrible silence while she shuffles into the centre of the room, accompanied by the rank smell of stale urine. She stops in the empty space in front of the stove and looks from me to Ma and back to me.

She gathers every scrap of air in the room into her ancient lungs.

"Because he's dead," she coughs, jabbing at me with a purple finger. "Dead, dead, DEAD!" The words echo from the walls. Behind me Poll gasps and Beatty whimpers.

"No," I say. "That can't be true, I saw him——"

Grandma stops me with her hand held high. She lumps herself on to a chair and surveys her audience. A horrible grin breaks over her crumpled old face. "Mrs Love's just found the devil in his kitchen – and he's dead as a doornail. Lying in a pool of blood. Murdered!"

"What?!" My voice rings in the silent kitchen.

"I expect he was murdered by fiends," says Grandma. "Demons sent by God to do Satan's work against the diabolical."

"That doesn't even make sense," mutters Beatty.

"Hush, devil child," says Grandma.

I turn to face her. Her horrible smile stretches from ear to ear. "But that can't possibly be true!"

"Oh it is, boy," she says, lumbering right up close and breathing her dead breath over me. "It's true, all right. What are you going to do now, eh?"

Chapter 3

It takes only a second for me to abandon the kitchen and get away from Grandma and her stink. I find the street's full of gawpers, and Mr Chen's door's open, and I can hear Mrs Love's voice holding forth over their heads. I turn and walk fast down the hill, away from his house.

I don't want to see anything.

I don't want it to be true. Something drips on my hands and I realise I'm crying. Stopping in the doorway of the Griffin I wipe my face on my sleeve, sniff away my tears and tuck the parcel under my arm before turning back up the street. If my collar's pulled up, perhaps no one will see my face.

"He'd have been the last person to see him alive," says a voice. "Athan Wilde."

I stare, and realise that the crowd of people outside Mr Chen's house are staring back at me.

"Me?" I say.

"Yes — you," says Mrs Love. "You knew all his business, didn't you? You worked for him."

"Did he?" says someone.

"Worked for the old man? Really?" says someone else.

"Don't be daft," says a soft, northern voice. "He's just a boy. He won't know anything."

There's a general murmur of agreement and the crowd turn away from me and go back to peering into Mr Chen's front door.

It's true. I probably was the last person to see him alive.

Except for his murderer.

I turn into New King Street and stop outside the Clay house.

All I can think about while I knock on the door is Mr Chen's smiling face. How could anyone murder him?

"Yes? What is it?" A dark-faced girl no older than I am stands in the doorway tapping her foot impatiently.

"Oh – it's you."

I shake Mr Chen away and pin my best smile to my face. "Mary, a parcel for – Mr K –?" The letters on the package wriggle and flex. I can't read it. "He lives here now?"

"Katz," she says in disgust. She holds out her hand. "Hand it over."

I shake my head and clutch the parcel close to my chest. "I need the money first or Ma'll have my guts."

"Well, you can't come in," she says, looking at me as if she's found me on the sole of her shoe. "You'll just have to wait there." She points at the front step, turns and slams the door in my face.

I'm not surprised. She hasn't really forgiven me for stealing a pudding from the kitchen table last year. It was a dare. It was also a very good pudding.

I sit back, leaning against the door. I try really hard not to think of Mr Chen, but then the windows across the road catch my eye and all I can do is remember last night. The magic. The engine.

And a little spark of anger lights. I'd like to know who did it. I'd like to...

Behind me the door springs open. It's not Mary. This time it's a pockmarked woman. She's very short, barely reaching my chest, and not once does she look up.

"Ten shillings," I say.

She drops ten shillings into my palm and vanishes back inside without a word.

The door slams, and I hear the bolts shoot across inside.

"It's as if he knew. As if he was expecting to be murdered. Before I left he gave me four sovereigns, *just in case*," I say to Tod Ballon, when we meet on the rooftops hours later.

I haven't cried again about Mr Chen and now I'm just angry. Angry and thinking. Angry that anyone could think of murdering such a gentle, intelligent man. And I'm thinking about finishing what he started, but I need Tod's help so now we're lying on our favourite building, with our feet in the gully, our backs on the slates, staring up at the moon. Side-by-side.

It's good up here. Private.

Below us the city's asleep. Except for all the things that aren't. The nightmen and their horses clatter trucks through the streets, emptying the cesspits. Flying things settle on chimneys and window sills around us. Small creeping things scrape their claws on the slates. Someone drags something across the floor in the room below us.

"Thing is, Tod, we were close, nearly there. We got the engine started last night."

"Is that what all the glass was about?"

"Yes," I laugh, remembering the fan spinning across the road and into the shop window. "He showed me how to put it together and it works." I sit up. "The engine works."

"You mean without a man or a horse or anything?"

I nod. "Just some oil and the electric box. It's like magic. Although he didn't like the word magic – he called it science."

Tod whistles again.

"But I need your help, to finish it and to fly it."

"What do you need me for then? I don't know anything about magical engines."

"You're clever with wood. I can't do that stuff on my own – you'd make it quick and strong."

Tod lets out a long sigh. "Flattery," he says. "Might work on some."

"Oh go on, Tod – you know you want to."

"So half of it's in the cellar, and the rest's on the roof?"

"It is," I say. It was a month ago when Tod and I dragged the wings of the machine through a hole in the ceiling and out of a skylight on to the church tower. "I hope no one goes to check the church bells.

But even with one half in one place and the rest in another, it's only a spit away from flying." I don't tell Tod that I don't know how to launch it. I mean, how difficult can that be?

"Do you know how the whole thing goes together?"

"Mostly," I say. I've been trying to remember all the elements of the machine. The engine, the fuel, the electric box and the bird herself. And where they all are.

And where Mr Chen hid the plans.

"He never told me where he kept his drawings, but if I can get all the pieces we can fiddle about with it till it works."

"Ah," says Tod. "Haddock's going to auction all of Chen's stuff tomorrow. I've got to help him bring everything out of the house. You could buy it all with your four sovereigns."

A tiny cloud crosses the moon and I imagine Mr Chen's things lugged out on to the street. The fan, and the engine, and the electric box, full of acid. I also imagine three of the four sovereigns, now safely tucked away in Polly's purse. She'd probably give them back.

"I wonder," I say. "If I drew them, do you think you could 'lose' one or two things?"

"You mean, one or two things could get forgotten

or left on the roof?"

"Exactly," I say. "And then you could help me finish it!"

"Course," he says, as if he's already agreed.

"*And* the henhouse?"

"The henhouse? What's that got to do with it?"

"It'd make Ma happy — or at least happier," I say.

"And the henhouse, and then we'll rule the world," says Tod, standing up and dancing half a jig on the ridge. "Athan Wilde — Fly Boy. Tod Ballon — Builder Extraordinaire. They are Kings of the City! Yay!" He stamps his feet, jumps into the air and vanishes.

"Tod?" I shout down. "Tod!"

Stumbling on to my stomach I lean over the top of the roof. There's no parapet on the far side, just a long black hole into nothing.

"Tod?"

"Athan." His voice comes from not very far away, but sounds strangled. "Help!"

Carefully I slide down the roof, resting my toes in the gutter on the far side. "Where are you?"

"Here!" he replies, his voice coming from just below my feet. I crouch, putting far too much of my weight in the gutter and look down between my ankles. I can see the top of Tod's curly head but the rest is too murky to make out.

"What's holding you up?" I ask.

"I am!" says a deep voice from below.

"Help," says Tod again. "He's got his hands around my neck."

"And I will drop him unless you promise never to climb on my roof at night again," says the voice. "You've woken me every night for years and years and I can't stand any more of it."

"I promise," says Tod.

"And you up there?" asks the voice. "Do you promise?"

"I promise," I say, with my fingers crossed behind my back. "On the life of my sister Beatty, I promise."

I'm up before the others in the morning. Up before Ma, up before Grandma can start mixing her incantations with her prayers but not up before Mr Haddock and Tod start to empty the house opposite.

I nip out, have a gentle word with Tod, slip him some drawings of what to look for, tip my hat to Mr Haddock and go back indoors. Even after a few minutes outside I have to hold my fingers under my armpits to warm up and I wonder at Tod, who seems unaware of the cold.

But he's tough. His dad's mean. A brute. Everyone, even Ma, is scared of him. He's gloomy and he drinks and he works in the coffin yard, building boxes for dead people. Ma's got a sharp tongue but Tod's father's handy with his belt.

I coax the little fire in the grate so that the shop goes from icy to cold, and sweep yesterday's dust balls into the ash.

Then I busy myself in the shop. Uncle's replaced the glass in the window, so I pretend to clean it, wiping off the smears of putty and then, when I can't pretend any longer, I take down the bolts of cloth from the shelves and roll and reroll them.

Footsteps sound upstairs. Probably Poll.

Without actually pressing my face to the glass and staring like a pig I watch the dawn light falling on the stuff outside.

Polly comes down to join me, both of us staring out at Mr Chen's things. As the sun rises, bright colours shine out of the darkness, spilling over the road; grass green, gold, purples and sea blues. Rich enamels, tapestries, embroidered silk cushions all jumbled together on drugget sheets keeping them from the dirt. Heaped on top, lacquer tables and chairs, themselves draped with more patterned fabrics. The whole of Mr Chen's house is out there.

Almost.

"There ought to be something good," says Polly.

"Some silks for us."

I nod, searching the heaps for anything from our machine, but so far Tod seems to have done well. I wonder how he hid the electric box.

People begin to drift out of their houses, assembling in little crowds on the street. A man with a brush and a pot of glue tries to paste numbers on the larger objects. He's struggling with a huge globe that's spinning wildly in the middle of the street, but it's all lopsided because it's been dumped on a pile of maps and leather-bound books, and his feet are sliding around on the books and there's paper flying all over the street.

Polly presses one of my sovereigns and six shillings into my hand. "Go and take a look at those silks, over there." She points at a heap by the globe. "If there's more than a few yards of one colour, we'll have it for linings."

Giving me the excuse I need, she stuffs me out through the door and I scoot around peering under the piles and inside the cabinets, pretending to look for silk.

As soon as the team stop lugging things out of the house, Mr Haddock the auctioneer scrambles up on to the back of a carriage, sporting a leery green jacket and begins the auction.

For a man made of gristle, he's got a lovely warm voice that reaches up and down the street and into some of the houses. Within a minute he's in full flight, while by his side Tod wobbles under the weight of a massive green bowl.

"What am I bid? Ladies and gentlemen, who'll chance a price? A magnificent example of eastern skill and quality!" he bellows across the sea of objects.

Avoiding the crowds, I check through the piles, stopping at the boxes from Mr Chen's larder. In fact they've only brought out the dried fruits and spices; they've left the all the chemicals behind. I point and wink at Tod, he winks back and his little finger gestures towards the house.

Beneath some pans, I find a bundle of cloth lying on the drugget, glowing like fresh spring grass, bright in the gloom of the street. A breeze catches it and a tiny sail billows along the selvedge. It might do for Polly. It might take Ma's mind off rooftops.

"*Western winds, when wilt thou blow...*" Not far away, Columbine Good's picking her way through the stuff, muttering and singing. A circle clears around her.

"*...the small rain down does fall, would my love were in my arms...*" Strange tufts of reddish hair cover her head, and half a bonnet dangles around her neck. They all think she's mad and they'd be right. Rumour says that she fell in love with our father, but he loved Ma. Then she fell for a soldier and was jilted at the altar. That she had a child that died. That she never recovered.

She gets on with Grandma. They worship the same mix of superstition and witchcraft but Ma can't abide her. It goes way back.

I'm never sure what I think about her.

The crowd shuffles and closes in, forcing Columbine out through the back. She droops against the wall and looks surprised before wandering off towards the Griffin Inn.

A nearby couple catch my eye. An odd pair, they're picking their way through the piles and junk and material as if they're looking for something.

She's what Ma might call a lady. She might once have been pretty, but she's frowned once too often and the wind has changed leaving a sharp face. Handsome, but sharp.

Her dress is perfect. Perfect cut, perfect stitch, perfect embroidery. She looks as if she's got money and plenty of it, which means that she doesn't fit round here at all. In fact, she's tucked her delicate gloved hand close to the arm of the man she's with as if the rest of us might eat her. I don't suppose she's ever been over here, among us grubby people.

The man's well kitted out. Dressed in a broadcloth

coat trimmed with blue, he's tall and grey-whiskered with huge shoulders, like a man who has worked for his living. He doesn't look the equal of the lady; he's rougher, coarser, more like us. It's the way he stands, and the battered sword, and the knife in his boot.

He's not really a gentleman even if he's pretending he is.

"Come, ladies and sirs, you must be able to see the beauty in these glorious receptacles…"

A dog raises its leg on a bale of linen and the sharp woman jabs it with her umbrella.

Someone bids for the green bowls and Tod clunks them on to a dresser top, rubbing his arms. He slips me a grin and shrinks back into the piles of junk.

Another lad takes over. Tod vanishes. Mr Haddock sells the globe, a stuffed bird and a mahogany bedstead.

The rain starts, darkening the silks, dulling the embroideries. The sharp woman puts up her umbrella.

"You all right there?" Tod stands at my side. He holds up an umbrella with two spokes and barely any cloth.

"You did well," I say. "No sign of the machine anywhere here."

"S'all safely tucked away inside."

"Where?"

"Here and there. You just need to get in the house

later to pick it up. How are you going to get it out?"

I ignore him as Mr Haddock starts off again. "And lot 271, a fine example of the Orient. This emerald fabric, a length of grass green to grace any fair lady, beauteous silks of India or Japan, a gown or bed linen perhaps?"

"That's mine," I say, moving myself into line with Mr Haddock.

"Young man – do I hear a shilling bid?"

I put up my hand.

"A shilling, we are bid by the ... young fellow to my left."

Nobody else moves.

I'm going to get it for a shilling.

"Two," he says, pointing at the sharp woman.

I stick my hand up again.

"Three," says Mr Haddock.

Quickly, she raises her hand. This time the man beside her turns to look at me. His face is scarred and dark with pox and whiskers, but his eyes are ice blue. He looks right through me.

He swings back and shares a joke with the woman.

"Four," says Mr Haddock, bowing to the woman. She bows back.

"Go on then," whispers Tod. "Five?" He jogs my elbow up to make the bid.

The woman holds up six fingers. She's laughing.

"Six," shouts Mr Haddock.

I glance towards the woman. Her face holds a pinched little smile. She doesn't want the cloth. She's playing a game – she just wants to bid against me, stop me getting it. The scarred man laughs too.

"Seven," I say, oddly angry and, for some reason, slightly scared.

The woman waves a glove at Mr Haddock.

"Does that mean she's stopped?" asks Tod.

"Seven shillings to the young man over there!" Mr Haddock slams his hammer down on a chest of drawers.

My face flushes. I've done it. I've bought Polly a big pile of cloth; there must be yards in that bundle. It'll pay for itself over and again.

"Well done!" says Tod. "I've never bought nothing at an auction."

I pat my pocket. Six shillings of Polly's and one of mine; nineteen shillings left.

"Pay now, boy – over by the clerk." Mr Haddock leans down from his cart and points towards a man sitting behind a table filling in a ledger.

"Held your nerve then, lad?" A soft voice at my ear makes me jump. The same northern tones I heard outside Mr Chen's house yesterday morning. The voice that called me "just a boy". I look up. The scarred stranger stands beside me, holding a purse. "Some fine kit in this sale, for them as have an idea of what they wants."

I freeze.

He winks at me.

The breath stops in my throat.

For a second I hear blood pumping in my ears and think it's drums.

Then I throw my coins on the table, grab the cloth and run.

Chapter 4

Tod helps me get the silk back into the shop. I slam the door and lock it. A thick smell of fresh bread and old soup fills the air.

"He was a bit terrifying, wasn't he?" says Tod.

"Not joking!" I reply. An imaginary hand touches my spine and I shiver and feel glad that there's a door between us and him.

"How you going to get the stuff I hid out of the house before Mrs Love rents it out again?" asks Tod.

"I've an idea," I say. "I think there's a way."

"Dinner, Tod?" asks Ma as we burst into the kitchen.

She smiles at him but looks right past me. I don't know if she's still angry about the rooftops or perhaps she's found something else to be cross about.

"This looks good, Athan." Polly drags the green silk over to the window.

The rest of us sit down. Tod and I settle at the other end from Ma.

Grandma says grace.

"For the multitudinous curses that are heaped upon this household, we ask forgiveness, oh Lord. From the duplicitous changeling child in our midst we ask release; for the idiot boy, we ask sense; and for the pig that gave its life that we might eat, we give thanks. Amen."

Polly unravels the cloth.

"Pretty colour," says Beatty.

"Loads of it too," I say, helping myself to a bowl of broth.

"How much d'you pay?" says Grandma. She shifts in her chair. I guess it's to cover a fart and, sure enough, a cabbagey smell soon drifts across the room.

"Seven shillings," I say.

"Seven shillings? For that heathen's stuff? Shocking!" She sucks on her soup spoon. She's almost toothless except for one long yellow fang at the front. "Green's unlucky, only the Irish and the fairies wear it." She pauses to fart again. "The saints never wore green," she says with certainty.

Polly's still sitting on the floor, the silk spread out around her. "Beautiful silk, but what's this, Athan?" She holds up a handful of the cloth, a thin bamboo stick caught up in it.

"What?" I say, and pull at the stick. It's attached.

"And another, and more…" she says, pulling the cloth through her arms.

Ma crosses to Polly and together they stretch out the cloth. It's not a roll, as I thought, it's a huge triangle with a bundle of sticks glued to it. In fact there are more sticks than fabric.

It's Mr Chen's flying machine. Not the real one, but the first one he made. He said it wouldn't fly and now the silk's glued to the canes, it's no good for lining coats.

"Oooh!" says Tod.

"Idiot," says Grandma.

"What is it?" asks Beatty.

"Nothing," Tod and I say together.

"I'll take it away," I say, grabbing it from Polly. "Pay you back." She stares at me, mystified, and I bundle the cloth and drag it through to the yard door and out to the henhouse.

When I come back in, Tod is still sitting at the table

and I can see the giggles burning up through his face. He's trying to hang on to himself, but a little like Grandma's farts the laughter won't be contained. I'd laugh too if I wasn't cross.

"So has Mrs Love asked if Uncle can clean up Mr Chen's house," I say, kicking him under the table, which just sends him into more shudders of silent laughter.

Ma takes her time to answer. "She has, as a matter of fact."

"Can I help him?" I say.

Ma slices a piece of Cheddar from the block. "It's not a gem of a job – don't expect he'll be able to pay you much. He's doing it tonight."

"But it's the house where Mr Chen died horribly, with spikes through his heart," Beatty says.

"D'you know that?" I say.

"She's making it up," says Polly.

"That's what she said," Beatty points at Grandma.

"Stuff, stuff," says Grandma, flapping Beatty away. "Devil child."

Chapter 5

The stories about Mr Chen's death ring in my ears. "He was strangled, throttled by his own guts." "Run through with the devil's pitchfork." "Kept alive by imps for three days, skewer'd to the ground." Grandma and mad Columbine Good came up with most of it. Ma went out to do some measuring and Grandma let Columbine in through the back door. They sat by the stove and whispered to each other — inventing horrors over some disgusting brew of Columbine's that's supposed to help Grandma's old joints.

"Murdered by Beelzebub himself, roasted in the fires of hell and rubbed in the quicklime of purgatory, before putting his head on a spike," hissed Columbine.

"Left hanging from the meat hook, a pentangle marked out in hen's blood beneath his feet on the holy book," suggested Grandma.

"Boiled in bile and roasted on a skeleton!" screamed Columbine.

They laughed and cackled and hooted. And Grandma laughed louder and wasn't a bit sorry for scaring Beatty and upsetting Polly.

I know it's all invented rubbish, but I half expect to find Mr Chen's tortured body in his kitchen. Instead there's a hurricane mess of boxes and packing, broken china and cobwebs. I'm leaning over a large sheet of wood that covers up a dark stain on the flagstones when Uncle touches my shoulder, making me jump.

"Come up, boy, we'll start at the top, sort this out later." I follow him up the narrow stairs. Like Ma, Uncle's as wide as two men and he jams on the corners. Both of us carry buckets, mops and plenty of Ma's tea leaves. By the time we've reached the top floor he's panting and has to sit down to loosen his neckerchief and suck in some air.

He waves his hand across his face as if to get more of a breeze. The house seems chill to me; each hollow step just proving how cold and empty it is.

I hadn't expected that.

"Tall, these houses. Not used to it, not used to it." His cheeks turn from purple to white. "When I was a nipper, they was just being built – used to run all over the building site with the foreman shouting at us. Just like you and your friend Tod." He winks.

"Ma told you?" I say.

"She has. I've told her it's high spirits but she's still hopping mad with you both." He heaves himself up and after scattering the tea leaves across the floor to gather the dust, begins to sweep away the shadows of Mr Chen's rugs and furniture.

I glance up at the trap door we made in the ceiling for the wings of the machine. It seems untouched, and I know that the cloth part is still out there. It'll have to stay there for now.

Instead I shuffle the dirt into piles and from those into waiting pails and lug them down the stairs, checking cupboards and nooks and crannies on my way.

Pieces of the machine are scattered all through the building, and on each trip I take a little time to run across the road and drop them over the wall into our yard alongside the hens. I lower the big brass engine down among them with a tatty shawl and they peck at it, their beaks ringing on the metal.

We move down the house, scouring and collecting

on our way. On the second floor, in a wall cupboard, I find some fire sticks, two jars of scarlet dye and a pile of folded paper birds. Nothing to do with the machine, but I pocket them. Beatty'll like the birds. Polly'll like the dye.

"Athan boy, spot of dinner?" Uncle calls up the stairs. "Come down a floor." I trot down the staircase to find Uncle leaning heavily on the wall, his shirt damp with sweat. I'm still cold.

He drops an onion into my palm. I settle by his feet and begin to gnaw at it.

Uncle wipes his mouth with a handkerchief, then says in a quiet voice that echoes around the empty room, "Your Gran'ma's asks me to get you a job. Seeing as Mr C's dead."

"Has she?" I peel a layer from the onion.

"With the nightmen."

"What?" I drop my onion and it rolls across the floor. "The nightmen?"

"Yep." He won't look me in the eye. "'Fraid so."

"She won't, Ma won't ... surely?"

He looks down at his onion as if it was very interesting.

The nightmen are the sewage clearers. They travel in foul wagons that go around in the night, stinking, splatting all over the roads collecting up the contents of the cess pools and privy pits. They're only allowed to clear the pits at night, so that the roads are clear of the smell during the day, but the rumours of half-dead white-faced madmen were the fuel of my childhood nightmares. For months Grandma said there was one living at the bottom of the stairs, that he'd eat me alive if I came down and bothered Ma in the evenings.

I believed her until Polly told me it was rubbish. I must have been about seven years old.

"A nightman?"

Uncle nods.

The nightmen don't even live in the town, they live out by their seeping ponds.

I sit and stare at the wall.

"I'm sorry." He stands up, his belly blocking out the light. "You're going to have to join them, boy, if you haven't got better work by the new year."

"Can't you wait until the summer? I'll have something by then."

He pulls a string of cobwebs from the shutters. "It's what your ma and grandma want. There's no more to be said." He sighs, as if real life is exhausting. "Come on now, up you get. This horrible house won't clean itself." He sets off down the stairs to get more water.

Chapter 6

I clean and I search and I try to think of a way of not being a nightman. There must be other Mr Chens out there. Other people who believe in science. People who need a handy boy around. While I think, I peer under every shelf, beneath every loose floorboard, checking for the plans.

By the time I reach Mr Chen's kitchen, night's almost set in. Uncle's taken all the rubbish and shoved it into his wagon standing out front. He's even stripped the bottles from the larder. I look up. There's no sign of the oil of vitriol, but the electric box is still there, lurking on the top shelf. Grabbing a stool from the wagon, I slowly lower it.

With it hanging low between my knees I stagger over the road, and with all my strength lift it on to the wall behind our yard, nestling the blackthorn around it. It's black and dirty. Hopefully no one'll notice it above their heads.

"Boy?" Uncle's voice rings over the empty street.

"Here," I call, racing back across the road.

"Thought you'd run off," he says.

I follow him back down the stairs.

In the kitchen there's nothing except for that pool of black between the hearth stone and the fire. I walk around it. I can guess what it is.

A small knot of fear forms near my heart as once again the rumours clamour and awful fire and brimstone images invade my head. Long shadows hide the corners of the room. It smells of Mr Chen's experiments, and ginger and sulphur – just as it should. But something else too. It smells of the butcher's.

Uncle whistles noisily. I join in, and we clean, picking the dark stain from between the flagstones, washing and scrubbing with soap and soda until the cracks are clean and the smell's gone. Only then do we stop whistling.

"Glad that's done. Bad – horrible way to go." Uncle points at the back door. "I've a little job for you outside."

He undoes the bolt and pushes me into the darkened yard. To the west under the clouds, a slash of rose-green sky still glows. Above that, night.

"Privy next." He claps me on the back. "Lovely job, bit of practice."

"Really?"

Uncle laughs. "You're not digging it out, not the muck – Mrs Love'll get the proper nightmen to come and do that. She just wants it mopped up a bit."

"What will *you* be doing?"

"Polishing the taps." He looks at me, a little smile on his broad face. "Surely you're not scared of a bit of manure, boy?"

As I step into the yard, my lantern flickers. No one's cleaned out this yard for a very long time. Things crunch under my feet and other things slither off to darker corners. I'm not scared, as such, but I don't much like deep shadows.

The lantern light plays across the walls and as I get closer to the privy door, my shadow shrinks. I stop with my hand on the latch, unsettled by the flickering and rustling of the yard creatures.

I've never much liked the dark places. Grandma used to shut me in the cupboard in her bedroom when I misbehaved. Which I did all the time.

According to her.

Back in the house I can hear Uncle climbing the stairs and I take a deep breath and pull the door open.

It stinks, but then all privies stink.

I check the eaves for the plans but there's no sign, and I realise that if they aren't in here, it may be that they've come out of the house and on to the wagon already. But I'd have seen them. Surely?

I lift the cover of the privy and place my lantern on the hook in the ceiling, so that I can see just enough but not too much. The smell almost makes me vomit, but I gulp it back and breathe thinly through my mouth. Armed with a bucket and plenty of soda I wash and mop and sluice. Then I lift the seat to peer underneath. Blackness. Then, just to be sure, I take the lantern from the hook and look down into the drop. The smell catches in my throat and I choke. Staggering back to breathe outside the door I knock my elbow on the doorframe and the lantern slips through my fingers and down the hole.

"Strewth!" Those big lanterns cost ten shillings each. I squint down the hideous pit.

It's resting on something vile and brown.

I'll have to get it back.

Out in the yard, I fumble about in search of anything I can use to fetch it out. I need to be quick or the flame'll die and I'll never find it.

From the doorway of the kitchen I spot a window hook. I take it and fish down the hole, hooking the lamp on my second go. As I bring it to the surface, my eye catches sight of a round shape lodged in the side of the pit. I hold the light next to it. It almost looks like a pipe, but not quite. It looks more hidden than built.

Oh! Mr Chen, you clever man.

Moving smoothly I bring the lamp to the top and hang it above me on the hook so that the whole space is dimly lit. I lean forward to look down.

Even with the light shining above, I can just make out where the shape is tucked into the side. It's no more than an arm's length but spattered all round with stink.

If I take off my shirt and jacket and take shallow breaths, I can reach down to that thing. If Mr Chen put it there, then I can get it out no matter how disgusting.

With my chest bare, I stretch my arm down the privy pit, and my head gets closer and closer to the seat, and the stench. My fingers brush the cold slimy sides of the pit before I can feel something different.

Oil cloth?

Flakes of something fall around my wrist, I can't see

them but I can guess what they are. Gently I close my hand around the thing in the side of the pit. It's cold, hard, damp. It feels like a ball. A wrapped-up ball.

Back in the yard, I fill a bucket with clean water and wash myself, the lamp and the packet. I dry myself with my already filthy shirt and put it back on. The shirt's damp; my skin's damp and goose pimples rise as I rub the coarse linen over it. I drag my jacket on and examine the parcel's wrappings in the lantern light.

"Athan boy?" Uncle stands at the kitchen door, peering out into the yard.

Pulling my woollen jacket over the top I slip the damp packet under my armpit. It's heavy and it slides around but I find if I clamp my elbow by my side I can keep it steady.

"Here," I say.

"All done?" he shouts.

"All done," I reply.

"Let's get out of this godforsaken house." Uncle's loaded everything on to his cart outside the front of the house. "Tell your ma I'll be round later on – I'll just get rid of this lot." He stops to survey me in the near blackness. "S'teeth, boy, look at you, you been swimming in it?"

Chapter 7

The moment I enter the shop Ma grabs me by the wrist and drags me down to the kitchen.

She must have been waiting for me.

"Go on, more!" she shouts at Polly, who tips steaming water into the large tub Ma uses as a dye bath.

"You pong, Athan," says Beatty from her stool.

I throw the folded birds at her. "Here — you can have these. Maybe you can make some more."

Ma pulls at my jacket. "It's all right, Ma, I can manage." I clamp my armpit hard to keep the oilskin parcel safe.

"Told you he'd stink," says Ma, her face screwed up.

She's right. I do stink. And after only one privy. One hour.

"Ma, is it a fact about the nightmen?" I ask. "Are you sending me to work with them?"

Polly and Ma swap looks.

"Who told you that?" Ma asks.

"Uncle says."

She takes a deep breath. "I'm not proud of it, but you have to pay your way. You've got till new year to find something better."

I open my mouth to argue, but Polly hisses at me so instead I dive for the back door. "I'll take my clothes off in the yard if they smell that bad." Moving crabwise so that they can't see the parcel, I shake off the jacket, keeping the ball inside the lining, and leave them both on the ground in the yard.

It would be icy cold, but the ground's coated in the hen straw, which crunches under my feet and around my ankles. I take off almost all my clothes and stand shivering, using the dark to try and get the wrappings off the ball.

"Hurry up!" yells Ma.

"Yes, I'm just trying to undo my breeches." My fingers slip on the oilcloth and, partly because of the cold, but mostly because I can't see what I'm doing,

I fumble. Looking up, I can see the fog has a slight glow. So there is a moon, just not down here.

I try to find a way past the cloth to the object inside.

"Your bath's ready, monsieur," calls Polly from the door.

"Coming," I call.

Half frozen, in nothing but my underwear, I have another frantic go at the wrappings. My fingers catch on a thread and I tug it from the oilcloth.

"Come on, the water's getting cold – it took me ages to heat it."

I wrench at each stitch, until it gives way. "I'm not having a bath with you all watching."

"She's seen worse," says Ma, coming to the door. They can't see me, but the two of them are clear against the red glow of the kitchen.

It's taking forever to open this thing. At last, the final thread breaks and I reach into the wrappings. A small smooth sphere tumbles out. Free of stink and feeling like polished wood.

I hear more water pouring into the bath as I look about for something to hide it in. My hat? It's the only thing that doesn't smell. I thrust the ball inside and drop it just inside the door, leaning the fire sticks against the front, hoping they might act as camouflage.

Ma and Polly stand like a pair of jailers, their arms

crossed as I pass between them.

In spite of their protests, I keep my drawers on until the water's dirty enough to hide my privates.

They chat as they add hot water and scrub my hair and back.

"Keep still, Athan. You're such a wrigglebum." Ma slaps my hands away from my face and attacks my ears with a bar of hard soap.

The bath's so short that my knees stick yards out of the water if my feet are in it. The last time they got me in the bath was when Tod and I swam upriver all the way to the weir and nearly froze. It was too short then and if it wasn't for the hot water that pours over my head whenever it suits Polly, I'd die of cold now.

Ma bundles up her skirts and takes herself upstairs. "Just to give you your modesty, boy, I'll check on the fire."

"I'm glad you're having a bath, Athan," says Beatty, smoothing one of the paper birds flat. "You pong of cheese." She thinks a moment. "And pickle."

"Shhh," says Polly. "Give him his privacy." She picks Beatty from her stool and staggers over to Ma's sewing chair.

I scrub at the dirt under my nails. Polly comes back and pulls at my hair, twisting it behind my head into a plait.

"Did you know about Ma sending me to be a nightman?" I whisper.

She shrugs and pulls my hair harder.

"You did?"

Polly leans forward into the tub. She's got tears in her eyes. "I did," she hisses. "Of course I did. They made me swear not to tell you. Athan, I don't want you to go to be a nightman, I need you here, to help with Beatty and Ma and all of this." She waves her arms round the dark kitchen, where Beatty lies in the shadows folding and unfolding the birds from Mr Chen's house. "I need you."

I look up at her. Big tears race down her cheeks. She looks far older than her years. "Will they really do it?"

She stands up and lays a drying sheet over the stove. "Yes, I think they will." She turns back, new tears still fresh in her eyes but a bright smile on her face. She speaks so that Beatty can hear. "Anyway, if you get yourself dressed, there's a clean shirt and drawers behind the range. I'll go up to the parlour. You bring Beatty when you're ready. I've got a present for you."

Chapter 8

"Me, me." Beatty puts out her arms to be carried.

Dressed in a clean shirt and drawers, I run up the stairs, Beatty slung over my hip. On the way past my bedroom, I shove the ball, still in my hat, into my bedding.

"What you hiding?" asks Beatty.

"Nothing. None of your business." I kiss her and carry her into the parlour. It's warm, even steamy. Uncle's arrived while I've been washing, and he's been scrubbed too. His round cheeks are red. A newspaper lies on his knee.

Grandma dribbles in her chair, her mouth open in

sleep, an empty cider mug in her hand. That's why she's got no teeth.

Polly sits with a brown paper parcel on her lap.

"I know what it is," says Beatty. "It's a—"

"Don't you dare!" says Polly. She holds the parcel out to me.

Everyone falls silent. Uncle's hands lie on the newspaper. Ma sits up. Beatty's eyes glitter in the near darkness.

"Is it my birthday?" I ask, wondering.

"Is it?" Beatty asks Ma.

Ma looks confused. "Oh – I don't think so." She rubs her eyes. "I think he was born in the summer." She stares at me as if the date should be tattooed on my forehead.

"Here," says Polly.

I take the parcel and undo the string. The brown paper unfurls and something rolls on to the rug. Green and gold. I reach for it and hold it up. A jacket. With lapels, and hooks, and tiny neat pockets.

"Oh!" I say, silenced. No one ever gave me anything. "Oh!"

"Is that all the boy can say?" snorts Grandma, waking up.

"For me?" I say to Polly as I stroke the cloth. "But it's brocade, the silk..." I mean that the material must have cost a fortune.

"Go on, try it," she says, smiling. So I stand up and slip it on. It fits like a second skin. I pull my arms across my chest and thrust out my elbows.

"Oh my! Doesn't he look good?" Ma rocks back and forth in her chair and claps her hands together.

"Fine as a cow turd stuck with primroses," mumbles Grandma. "Much good it'll do him when he's cleaning out the cesspools."

Uncle looks over his spectacles at Grandma and raises an eyebrow.

The cloth stretches smoothly across my shoulders. I stand in the gleaming jacket and my drawers, turning before the fire. Happiness soaks through me. This is a proper jacket, a coat made with love and skill, not the clothes of someone who digs out the sewers. Surely Ma doesn't expect me to creep round the streets in the dark dressed like this.

"And these," says Polly, laughing and throwing a pair of buff corded silk breeches at me. I drag them on. I close the waist hooks and stand on my toes to see myself in the mirror above the fire. Someone else looks back at me. A smart young man, his hair in a plait, his collar open, his jacket loose.

"Me?" I say, asking the mirror. "Me?"

"Yes – you," squeals Beatty. "Shall I tell you a story?

It's about a boy who falls in love with his ref-el-ction and drowns in a pond. There was no one but a flower to save him." Her voice trembles on the last word. She gazes at me, then smiles and falls back to folding and unfolding one of the birds I found in Mr Chen's cupboard.

"Doesn't that fairy child ever think of anything but death," Grandma mutters.

"Shh, Grandma." Polly settles by Beatty and helps her make a new bird from a corner of newspaper.

The fire crackles and Uncle snores. "You're wasting the cloth, Molly." Grandma turns to Ma.

"For why?" Ma answers.

"Dressing him up like a parrot, when he's off to do dirty work. What a waste of good cloth."

"I'm giving him five weeks, Mother. He might yet find work with the Quality."

I wonder if they even remember I'm in the room.

"And it isn't right that that idiot boy should be so vain," Grandma shouts suddenly. Her face puckered. "He'll shatter the mirror if he goes on looking at himself like that, and if he does that, there'll be more bad luck in this house, seven years at the least." She leans back and crosses herself. Her lips form silent words.

Ma stares straight ahead. Polly sniffs.

"Eight years since the fairy child was born," says Grandma. "And eight since their father skipped off to who knows where without a by your leave."

"He went for adventure," says Polly.

"He went for the work," says Ma firmly.

"He went for the women," mutters Grandma.

Uncle holds up his newspaper. "They're offering a reward. A big one — ten thousand guineas."

"Who? What for?" asks Polly.

"First person to fly. It says here: *The Duke of Roseberry challenges anyone to fly over a distance of two miles, without recourse to the ground, using wings or power. Reward 10,000 guineas to the first proven flight.*"

I go cold. Then hot, then cold.

No one else notices.

"Ten thousand guineas?" I say.

Beatty holds up one of the folded birds and flaps the wings.

"'S'impossible, of course," says Uncle. "No one's ever going to claim it."

"Why would they want someone to fly?" asks Ma. "I mean, what use is that?"

"Ma?" Polly's mouth falls open. "You could cross the seas, and the mountains."

"Yes," I say. "You could." I watch the smoke curling up the chimney, thinking of the wooden ball hidden under my pillow and the kite on the church roof. And I wonder if Mr Chen knew about the reward. He probably did, he probably knew that someone else would want the flying machine to get the reward. But he wouldn't have wanted it himself. Mr Chen wasn't interested in money.

I feel Polly's hand on my shoulder. She pushes me towards the mirror. I gaze at our reflections. Her eyes are the same as mine, dark and wide, but where my hair's brown and ordinary, Polly's is copper beech, darkly red. It curls over her narrow shoulders like a fur.

"Can you win it for me, Athan?" she says. "With all Mr Chen's knowledge, you must be able to fly."

I stare into her eyes, but she doesn't know; she's mocking me.

I smile back, she squeezes my hand and whispers, "Find a good job, Athan. Find one tomorrow. Don't let them turn you into a nightman."

"Is that why you made these clothes?"

Polly nods. Her eyes swim and she turns away to sit on the sofa. The firelight flickers over her delicate face.

She's so thin. We all are, except for Ma and Uncle, who get fatter by the week. I don't know how they get fat on porridge, porridge and soup. I can see Polly's ribs beneath her dress. I glance across to Beatty. She's no more than bones and down. A chick.

10,000 guineas. What would 10,000 guineas do for us?

Uncle reaches for his fiddle. He uses his neckerchief to wipe off a thin layer of dust and begins a tune. He plays a dirge that breaks into a jig. A smile spreads over Polly's face and she curls sideways, her heavy shoe beating time to the music.

"Go get a jug of cider from the Griffin, boy, be a darling." Ma's chair creaks as she leans back.

"Oh, Ma, I'm lovely and warm at last. And my boots are in the yard."

"Take your uncle's."

"Oh, Ma," I plead. But I know she won't let it go, so I button my jacket, put on Uncle's boots and set off for the inn.

Chapter 9

Closing the door on the lights from our shop I step into darkness. Barely a glimmer shows behind the shutters in the other houses. The winter fog's rolling in from the river and, mixed with the coal smoke, it's spreading its blanket across the town. I pause to let my eyes get used to the darkness.

Something cold brushes my face. Snow? I grope past the front of the shop and around the block until I smell the cider from the Griffin.

The heavy door grates on the flagstones; I'm barely inside before Columbine Good shouts at me. "Shut the door!" She's sitting in the fireplace holding her skirts up to let the heat at her horrible legs. They're blue with veins and red with ulcers.

I close the door behind me and look about. There's hardly anyone in here. Only Columbine by the fire, and someone to the side I can hardly see. No sign of Peter, the landlord. I walk towards the cellar steps, ready to call down, when the person in the shadows catches my eye. All I can see is large knotted hands in a pool of candlelight cutting a yellow block of cheese into miniature cubes with a dagger. The hands arrange the cut yellow squares like soldiers on a slice of bread.

I watch as the hands pick up the slice and take it into the darkness where there must be a waiting mouth.

Behind me, by the fire, Columbine starts to sing.

"*Farewell ye dungeons dark and strong, farewell, farewell to thee...*"

"Someone shut her up!" Peter sticks his head up from the cellar.

Columbine takes no notice. "*...Macpherson's life shall not be long, on yonder gallows tree...*"

"Cider?" he asks.

I nod.

"Wait here, boy."

He dips back down to the cellar, and I sit on a chair.

"*... Sae wantonly, sae hauntingly, played he...*" Columbine's eyes close, and her head falls back; she's giving the song all she can. Her old voice cracks on the high notes and goes breathy on the low ones.

Then the owner of the hands steps out from darkness, rises to his feet, light as a cat, and tiptoes towards her. He halts and I see who it is. The scarred man from the auction. His grizzled head moves close to hers and I sit still, staring.

Columbine takes an age to reach the high note and I watch as his head gets closer and closer.

"...Be-low the gallows tree..."

He holds his hands out on either side of her neck. "Quiet, woman," he whispers.

Then he clamps her throat.

"Aaaah!" she screams, and grabs him.

He shakes her off and for a moment they stare at each other, his huge shaggy head no more than a hand's breadth from her red cheeks. Something crosses her features, a tiny glimpse of recognition, but as soon as it's there, it's gone and she slumps back against the wall and sips from a mug, her eyes dull with drink. When I look for the scarred man, he's back at his table, arranging his supper in neat lines.

It's as if it never happened.

He never looks up.

A clock ticks.

The fire steams and spits.

I keep my eyes on the floor.

Peter clanks downstairs. *Hurry up.*

I sit on the chair and fiddle with the binding on my jacket. I try to think good thoughts. But they keep on coming back to the man arranging cheese in the gloom and the blood on Mr Chen's kitchen floor.

"Come here then, lad."

I look around. There's no one else, he has to be talking to me. My skin prickles. "Yes, I'm talking to you." His voice is soft and dark. Definitely from the north.

"Sir?"

"Join me then."

I think about running and then I think about murder. I won't find out more if I don't stay.

Moving slowly, I slip into the settle opposite him. Eight squares of cheese face me. Above them the bright-blue eyes look out from the battered face. Not just pox, knife scars too.

"What's your name, lad?"

"Athan Wilde."

His eyebrows rise. "Fancy a bit of cheese?" He barely moves his mouth when he speaks, but his eyes dance.

"No, thank you."

"It's southern muck. The landlord says it's from

hereabouts." His mouth stretches into a grin. Rat's teeth with a single gold one, right in the middle at the front.

I pull my feet back as far as I can and keep my hands on the table top.

"Live round here, do you?" He leans back, and I see the buttons on his coat. Expensive, nice. "Did I see you come out of the tailor's shop?" He reaches across the table for a jug and swills his mouth round. "If I hadn't known, I should have guessed."

"Should you?" I ask.

"Aye – good clouts you're wearing there. Now. Not the togs you was wearing at the auction. I mean, I ask m'self, what's a boy like you doing dressed as a marquis, unless they've someone on the inside. I notice things, me."

So he does recognise me. I finger my jacket. It's fine, very fine. But so's his.

I stare at his cold eyes, his scarred face and his battered sword. If I keep staring, he might back down. I'm not going to let him know he scares me.

"So, if you come from round here, why don't you tell me about the old man, and while you're at it, who cleaned up the house today, after the auction, eh?" While he's talking, he slides to his feet, steps round the table and sits next to me. His arm rests against mine. His little pieces of cheese all lined up for attack.

The room's dead cold, but the sweat's breaking out on my palms and on the back of my neck. *Where's Peter?*

"Everything was sold at the auction, I swear." As I say it, my mind fills with pictures of Uncle's loaded cart and my own arm stretched deep down the privy.

He gazes at me, and I stare at his hands shuffling the cheese into new lines. There's a horrible long silence. I glance over to Columbine; she's watching us.

"Not that stuff. I don't mean the valuables. I mean the man's diaries, his accounts – the day to day of his living. Who's got that, eh?" The stranger's hand creeps over mine and holds it to the table. "A clever person'd share their secrets, they'd see their way to a few shillin's."

I watch the candle flame. I want to find out about Mr Chen's murder – he wants to find out about Mr Chen. So far, he's winning. "What's your interest in Mr Chen? Why do you want to know about him?" I ask it as casually as I can although my mouth is so dry the words barely make it past my teeth.

He presses his hand down a little harder. It's cold and hard as iron. "I've got some friends. Powerful, rich, clever friends as would like to know things the old man knew."

"Oh," I say, sounding bored. "But I don't know anything." He's so close I can feel his warmth.

"That's interesting." With his knife he skewers a square of cheese to the bench top.

I say nothing.

"Because," he lays his arm along my shoulders, pressing his cheek right next to mine, "a little bird told me that the old man had a lad working for him, a lad from the tailoring shop. And that lad, and his uncle, cleared up the 'ouse afterwards, that they would have found anything left and that this lad was a lad very like yourself."

"Boy!" shouts Peter from the steps.

The stranger lets go. Quick as mercury he stands by the table, his hand outstretched. "Nice to meet you, Athan. I'm sure our paths'll cross soon. Very soon."

He takes the jug from Peter, presses it into my hand and shoves me towards the door.

"Don't forget me, will ye? I won't forget you." He grins. "I promise."

Chapter 10

I run from the inn. My feet skid on the cobbles, and when I reach our house I throw myself inside and bolt the door. After pulling down the heavy shutters, I slip down the stairs to the kitchen and lock the yard door.

Only then do I run back upstairs with the cider. The room seems fine, it all seems ordinary. Ma and Uncle laugh and drink. Beatty's gone to bed, Polly's flicking through song sheets. In the room it's yellow and warm and safe.

Taking a stub of candle I step back on to the landing. The darkness seems darker. The cold colder.

After touring the house, checking the doors and

windows once more, I halt in the kitchen. Pressing my cheek against the glass, I peer into the dark yard. The snow's falling now, thick and fast. It's settling on the heap of silk, the makeshift henhouse, the sticks of rubbish I've collected from the builder's yards. There's no scarred stranger turning into a snowman in our yard. But the feeling that someone's walking down my spine happens again and again, until I'm shivering.

Is he still in the Griffin? Or waiting for me out there in the darkness, the snow landing on his horrible skin?

Back in my room, I sit on my bed and pull the sphere from under my pillow. By candlelight little ivory crescent moons shine white; between them, ebony stars. I slide my fingers over the surfaces of the different woods. There seems to be no way in, no join between top and bottom or side to side.

"Oh, Mr Chen," I say. "Why did you have to make it so difficult?"

Footsteps ring on the paving. Someone walking up the road. They stop outside the shop. I sneak to the window and peer through the grimy glass.

Snowflakes eddy in the darkness. A figure stands waiting.

It's him. I can see the sword.

He steps forward.

I wait.

The door handle of the shop clanks downstairs but I locked it behind me and the figure stays on the pavement, standing, staring up at the windows before shaking his head and walking on up the road.

I watch the corner, waiting for him to reappear, but the snow falls steadily and he stays away.

Raising the sash, I stick my head out of the window.

Outside, everything's white. Even the stranger's footprints have disappeared.

Almost silence. Only the faintest rustle as the snowflakes rest on each other, layer on layer smothering all the sounds of the city.

Closing the window, I watch the clock outside the shop.

I watch the street.

I listen to my heart. Slower, steadier.

Midnight. Perhaps I'm worrying over nothing. Perhaps he's just one of those people that likes to put the wind up people like me. He might have nothing to do with Mr Chen's murder. Though I've never seen him before today.

Polly goes to bed and Uncle's boots thump on the stairs.

"Night, Moll!" he shouts from the shop, and stamps out through the front door. I watch him roll down the street and turn off to leave the city. He'll pick his way down the frozen cart tracks, between the smoking rubbish heaps, to home.

I roll the ball across the bed.

10,000 guineas.

I'll have to find another job. Something, anything. A day job so that I can finish the bird and stop Ma sending me off to be a nightman. And maybe – just maybe – win that money.

A tiny avalanche of snow slips down past the window.

Tomorrow I'll go round, knock on the doors, present myself as a useful anything boy. Cleaning, messages, horses, hens, anything. It won't buy us peaches, but it would let me pay my way, and it would keep me around to help Polly and carry Beatty, and share the load with Grandma.

And then that would leave me the evenings to complete the machine.

My fingers play over the ball, turning it over and over in my hands, looking for a way in, a top or a bottom or a sliding drawer. It's like a block of wood, but it isn't solid. The grain runs in different directions, and the moons and stars seem to mark out a pattern. Ten moons, ten stars.

I thump about in my room, making the noises of bedtime as Ma hauls herself up the staircase. She stops on the landing, listens and goes on up. The moment she's passed, I break my promise. I sit on the window ledge and throw the sash up until a blast of freezing air fills my room.

Sticking the ball inside my coat, I pull myself up until I'm standing on the sill outside the window. It's very cold, and the snow's settling on my coat and head. If I could see the colour of my fingers, they'd be white.

I lower myself by my fingertips and drop down silently into the street. The snow's covered everything, sugar white, glistening. Pristine.

It crunches under my feet and I walk down the front of our shop and stop by our tall back wall. The electric box is still there, perched on the top, the blackthorn almost covering it, and I give myself a grin, knowing that the scarred stranger has walked straight past it without a clue.

I clamber on top of a crate and slither over the wall into our yard. The hens make little warm cheeping sounds.

"S'all right, girls, only me," I say. Gritting my teeth, I raise the electric box and lower it on to the chicken straw below. The wooden fan and the brass engine fit alongside nicely and I grab a piece of oilcloth and cover all three from the weather. I hope the snow hasn't done them any harm, but they weren't there for long. And they won't be, if I can just get Tod to give me a hand with them down to his loft.

Tod.

I look up.

Just to my left, the drainpipe runs down from the roof gully and I slip my arm around it to pull myself up to the parapet above. The metal is so cold, I burn my fingers touching it, but there's no other way to reach the roof, so I move as fast as I can, up through the cloud of smoke and soot coming from our chimney until I can roll over on to the gully.

Although the sky's thick with snowflakes, it's not completely dark. Somewhere up there the moon's shining, and if the clouds blow over, the city'll be astonishing.

The snow's settled thickly on the outer roof. Even the feeble trees that grow out of our gutter have snow piled on their little branches. I swing my leg over the front roof so that I reach the safe and secret gully between front and back. At the end of the gully, the neighbour's chimney stack rises into the whirling snowflakes. I've climbed it many times, and even though the ledges are icy, it's only a minute before I'm able to run along the roof tops all the way around to the square. From there, I slip down to the ground, scuttle past the Beaufort, across the gravel, and clamber up on to the big houses on the east side. I could walk on the ground, but the world's better from high up.

Up here the snow's blown itself against the chimney stacks, so that the roofs look tipsy – half bare, half snug in a white blanket. I stand and peer over the parapet. Through the snowflakes, I can see the street below, but it's unclear, as if the ground's a dream, or I'm a dream.

"Athan!" Tod appears behind me. He climbs over from the front roof then rests his chin on the ridge tiles.

"Look!" I say, pulling the sphere out of my coat.

"What's that?"

"It's the plans, I think, but I can't open it."

He stares. Because of the moon and the snow, I can see his face quite clearly. Black and white but light.

"Where'd you get it then? I looked all over."

"Mr Chen's privy."

"Get away?" Tod grabs it from my hand, twisting and turning. "Come on then. Can't be that difficult. Nothing's that difficult." He goes on turning it one way, then the other. His fingers dance over the inlay, the moons shine in the snowlight. I have a sudden thought.

"Try pressing the white bits as I turn it."

Ping. Like a flower it opens up.

"Blimey!" Tod looks up at me.

I reach my fingers inside, half expecting to have them bitten by some invention of Mr Chen's hidden in the darkness but instead meet the crackle of paper. I tug and a wedge of folded paper slowly emerges from the inside of the sphere.

A single snowflake falls and settles on my hand.

"Open it out," says Tod, holding his jacket over me.

It's thick paper. I unfold it, once, twice, three times. It becomes so big we have to hold it between us. But in the dark I can see nothing more than a large triangle marked out in ink.

"Are these the plans?" whispers Tod.

"Think so," I say. We stare at them in the snowlight.

"I don't understand most of it though," says Tod.

"I do," I say. "I think."

He peers over my shoulder, my fingers trace the lines, working out how the pieces join when, below us, I hear a sash go down.

We freeze.

"You're there again, aren't you?" shouts a man's voice. The same man who caught Tod by the neck a night or two back.

Tod stands, really slowly, but as he does, he knocks the chimney next to him and a blob of snow falls and whisks down the slope, tumbling off the roof to the street below.

"It's no good pretending you're not," says the voice.

Reaching my arm across the pitch of the roof I half stand.

"Well, you swore on the life of your sister, boy — remember that." And the sash slams down, shaking the whole building and sending snow cascading past us.

"He's got no sense of humour," says, Tod, cramming a handful of snow down my collar. He turns and runs straight back over the side of the house.

"Tod! Don't you..." I shout, and jamming the ball and the plans in my pocket I race him down across the frozen slush in the square and straight up another down pipe, more than five storeys up, until I see him break through the eddies of snow and suddenly the world becomes clear.

I drag myself over the parapet, hot under my jacket but with frozen fingers. Moonlight falls on the snow-covered tiles, showing the softened ridges. It all looks like a perfect world, black and white, no dead leaves, no dead seagulls. At our feet, mist fills the bottom of the town; above us, the black sky glitters with a million stars, and the air shimmers with cold. It's going to be a hard frost.

Tod slides down the roof and lies flat on his back on the snow. He's talking. "Glorious," he says. "Your grandma says the stars twinkle more in the cold; it's to show the way for the angels when they come to pick up the people who've died of cold in the ditches."

"Rubbish," I say.

I lie down beside him, slipping my hand back in my pocket, feeling the heavy wooden ball and the crunch of paper.

We sit in silence. Finally I tell Tod about the man from the auction, him being at the pub and threatening me.

We lie staring at the sky, thinking.

"Do you think he killed him?"

"I don't know," I reply. "He might just be a chancer, but he's scary, Tod. And I'm not easily scared."

Tod thinks for a while. "If he's going to make trouble, perhaps you should just give him what he wants?"

"Do you really think that?" I ask.

"No," says Tod after a while.

"Exactly," I say.

"You could burn the plans," says Tod. "Destroy everything that we know Mr Chen left behind. Then he can't get hold of it and it would be safe. Let some other gawney have a go at it."

"But there's a prize, Tod." I say. "Some lord or other's offering ten thousand guineas for the first person to fly."

"S'teeth, Athan! Are you thinking of going for it?" Tod rolls on to his stomach so that all I can see is a ring of shaggy hair.

"We, Tod, we! We're going for it." We both stare as a tiny cloud drops a handful of flakes across the moon. "We could win. Mr Chen knew that bamboo was light, like the hollow bones in bird's wings. He knew that the silk was strong and thin. I don't think anyone else has ever thought about that."

"You mean their machines are too heavy."

"That's what Mr Chen thought," I say, sitting up.

"Sounds a fine idea. I'm up for it," Todd says, stretching his legs behind him, and waving his arms, making a snow angel.

I grab at his legs, and he turns round to swipe me. I dance to one side and we skip across to the next house. Then we begin to run, jumping over the joins between the houses, landing on the slanted slates, two steps and on to the next roof, leaping and laughing, our arms outstretched, almost flying between the rooftops. Racing over the heads of the sleeping people inches below us.

Like birds.

Chapter 11

On the edge of sleep, I dream. I'm flying over the city. I skim the snowy tiles, I brush the chimney pots, but the streets are cold and empty.

I rise, breaking through the thick wool of cloud to breathe the clear night air. Up here it's so cold that my eyelashes freeze, but I want to play up here among the stars; they tempt me and the moon smiles, her mouth a wide, crooked grin.

I'm drawn back down by the city, and I drift until the lights spread out beneath me.

Beyond the city a lane winds westward. Between smoking bonfires I find a small collection of broken houses. By them, there is a pond, clogged with rubbish. Two white swans sleep still. Their heads tucked under their wings while silently a fox steals off with their cygnet. No one sees, no one hears, although I, high above, catch the reedy cry of alarm as the little bird gives up the struggle.

Behind a barn, two figures lit by a dim lantern rummage through a waggon. They are collecting paper, making crunching sounds. I dive low over their heads but so intent are they on searching that I pass them by.

They hear nothing but the faint rustle of wings.

An owl, they might think.

I circle again, breaking through the cloud, high, up towards the laughing moon. I breathe and plunge again.

I rise to drift up there on the rim of space and through a break in the cloud I see a heavy man walk back from the city. I need to see more, so I swoop until I can almost feel his breath. His path is unsteady as he weaves between the freezing ruts, and I hear him whistle. A cheerful tune that turns round and round itself like children playing.

He halts and challenges the men. Was that a knife I see? A blade of some sort?

A cry. The two men run.

I try to shout, but my words fly off in the wind. I watch as the heavy man sinks to the ground. I call to him, but my voice has gone, and anyway he cannot hear.

The men are almost back at the city.

I circle again. The man lies still on the ground.

The snow is white.

The snow is red.

I wake and even though I don't know why, I know I'm worried. I stare stupidly at the falling snow, trying to remember what I'm doing slumped by the window fully dressed.

That dream – the man on the ground. Red snow.

The pub, the scarred man.

The plans.

I pull the paper from my pocket. It's scattered with Mr Chen's writing. A mixture of words and drawings all surrounding that familiar shape of the arrow. The flying machine. The plan folds easily back into the sphere and I push the wooden petals closed until it clicks shut. I roll it back and forth across my bedcover, thinking of somewhere to hide it. It's awkward, too big to conceal under something. Tod's loft would be best, but for now it'll have to be in this house. I slip into the parlour and feel behind the top of the clock.

There's a wide ledge and I've used it before to hide things from Ma and Polly. It'll have to do again. The sphere rolls along and stops in the middle. From the front it's invisible and from the sides it blends into the mahogany clock case.

Downstairs I find Polly and Beatty at the kitchen table, sharing a cup of tea and whispering. Beatty's face is pale and crinkled with worry. There's no sign of Ma.

"What's happened?" I ask.

"Uncle's been nearly murdered," says Beatty. "It's the curse of Mr Chen, you know. Grandma says so – she says that because he was being a follower of Mephistopheles—"

"Ssshh, Beatty – that's not it, he's not been murdered," says Polly.

"What?" I ask, dreading the answer. I take a piece of orange peel and and crush it between my fingers. The kitchen fills with the sharp sweet smell.

"Well, this man came to the house, with Mrs Love—" starts Polly.

"He's going to rent Mr Chen's house from Mrs Love. Ma was thinking him ever so handsome. She put on a new dress, one she didn't wobble in," finishes Beatty.

Polly goes on, "And Ma gave him coffee, and while

he was here, Samuel Parfitt came to say that Uncle had been found near death on the road home."

"And the man took Ma over to Uncle's in a proper shiny carriage. He's a soldier, he's fought against the French and everywhere in the world, and he's called Colonel Blade. And that was hours ago."

I shake my head at them both. "But Uncle, what happened to Uncle?" I ask.

"They've stitched him up proper," says Beatty. "Like a pudding."

"Beatty!" says Polly. "Shhhh now."

"Do they know who did it?" I ask. I say the words, but somehow I know what happened. I've seen it.

"We don't know that, boy." Grandma shuffles down the stairs and into the kitchen. She holds her hands in front of the range and coughs like a horse. "Only the Lord knows that. Perhaps it was divine intervention, your uncle's part in that godless house across the road." She pauses and her eyes grow with thought. She glances over to Beatty. "Or perhaps it was the fairies." She helps herself to the last piece of bread and hoists herself back up the stairs, farting and groaning.

Polly looks at me. "What are you doing today?"

"Looking for a job. Beatty can come too." I hoist her on to my hip. "Would you like to come and help me find work?"

"Is the snow very deep?"

I shake my head.

"Then you can take me with you, Athan, and you can teach me to make snowballs."

"Deliver this to Mr Katz, will you?" Polly throws a parcel at me and a heavy coat of new blue wool. She rummages in the store cupboard. "Here, have these — they're Pa's. And this…"

She ties a silk cravat around my neck.

"Now don't come back till you've got a job."

Chapter 12

"Do you think they might be angels, Athan?" Beatty asks, holding her mittens up to the snowflakes circling around her head.

"Angels?" I ask, pulling the wheeled chair out of the gutter and skirting a large patch of ice. It's not very far to New King Street, but with Beatty flinging handfuls of snow into my face it feels like miles.

"Or the dead? Thousands of lost spirits, laid to rest at last?"

I laugh. "Mr Chen once told me that if you look under a glass, you can see that every snowflake has a different pattern. They're made of ice crystals, not angels."

A sedan chair goes past, carried by two men, swearing and red faced.

"Can you do that?" Beatty asks.

"I should think so." I watch the chairmen slide off around the corner. "It looks easy enough."

We've reached the house and I hammer on the door.

Mary answers. I brace myself for an insult but instead she smiles at me. I wonder if she might be pleased to see me.

"Is Mr Katz at home?" I ask.

"Indeed." She curtseys. "Hello, Beatty, how are you? Come up into the hallway – I'll ask him down."

"I'll wait here if I might. We've that chair." I point at the huge wheels of Beatty's chair, spotted with packed ice.

Mary waves at Beatty and vanishes up the stairs.

"She's extra pretty, you know she is, she's got chocolate eyes and caramel skin – lovely," Beatty giggles. "I 'spect you'll marry her next week, then she'll be taken 'way by a cloud devil and magicked into flowers."

"Beatty!"

Mary returns with a tall man with a long duck nose and a serious mouth. He's holding a thick piece of glass, rounded and polished.

"For my telescope," he says, a very slight smile on his lips.

I shake my head. I have no idea what a telescope is.

"I show you some time. On a clear night." I'm still staring at the glass when I realise that he's holding out some coins in his other hand.

"Oh – thank you," I say, taking the money as he heads towards the stairs.

"Excuse me, sir – have you any jobs going?"

He wanders back towards me. His eyes run over my clothes and my face and I feel well and truly examined. "What work have you done before?" he asks.

"I used to work for Mr Chen."

"Oh, how interesting – the one who––"

"Died horribly," Beatty yells from her chair behind me.

Mr Katz raises his eyebrows. "I might have. I will think on it." He dips his head in parting and walks back into the house.

I glance back up at Mary and she smiles. Beatty's right, she has dark-brown eyes, warm with flecks of black, like a fresh eel.

"I don't know if you'd want to work here. He's a bit odd," she says. "Plays music in the assembly rooms in the day, and makes things or stares at the sky all night. His sister's the same; they're from Germany."

"C'mon, Athan," says Beatty. "I want to play in the snow."

"Off you go then," says Mary. "Enjoy yourselves." She looks out at the street as if she'd like to play in the snow too, but she closes the door and I hear her footsteps clunk on the wooden boards.

"Can we go and see the people, Athan?" says Beatty, pulling the blanket over her arms.

"Really? You want to go into the middle of town?"

"I want to see the people. I never get to see the people. It's too far for Poll," she pleads.

It occurs to me that I might be able to get some oil of vitriol in town. Me and Tod are going to need it.

"All right then." I fight through the streets, pushing the wheeled chair. As we get closer, the pavements fill with traders slipping about.

We skim the market. Cabbage leaves spew from the back of a cart and catch the wind, barrelling down the street, bursting through the snowflakes and pasting themselves across the fish market. The Quality struggle out of the hot Baths into the blizzard, their hats close to their wigs, searching for sedan chairs while the traders call and haggle, ignoring them completely.

I can't help feeling there are two types of people in this town. Us and them.

Beatty points at a group of women, all wigged and

powdered, picking their way through the slush and market rubbish. Because of their silly shoes, they walk like ducks, sliding on the cobbles.

"Why do they come here?" Beatty asks.

I'd wondered this myself when I was little. "Because of the waters," I answer. "The waters are warm and healing. They cure people."

"Can't I go in them?" asks Beatty. "Can't I be cured?"

I shake my head. Beatty's legs can't be cured. There's nothing of them. It's as if she didn't really have any proper legs when she was born, but I can't say that to her. Instead, I say, "I think they're for rheumatics and gout and that kind of thing."

A small tear trickles down Beatty's cheek. She wipes it away with her red blanket but I see it before she does.

"Stop, I want to look there, please, Athan," she says, pointing at a shop to our right. Struggling over the cobbles, I heave the chair on to the pavement and drag it alongside the huge shop window. It's a fancy shop, it smells of sugar and violets. Tod and I have spent our lives staring hopelessly through the glass but this time, I actually have a little money in my pocket.

"Oh!" Beatty draws in her breath.

It glows and it glitters. More so with the snow falling around our heads. Inside the window, golden trays on mirrored shelves, heaped with sugar mice, and liquorice, and chocolates dusted with sugar. Marzipan fruits, and candied orange cluster together with a pile of glacé cherries.

"Oh," she says again.

I reach into my pocket. It's heavy with coins, although I was going to spend them on chemicals.

A couple of sugar mice wouldn't hurt.

"Stay here," I say.

"I might grow wings and fly away," she says.

Kicking the pads of snow from my feet I push the door open and stand on the mat watching the ice crystals melt off my shoes. The shop is warm and smells richly sweet, hot caramel and oranges thickening the air.

"Sir?" says the woman behind the counter.

I look around and realise she's talking to me. "Oh – two sugar mice, if you please. And two of those red things." I point into the window. Through the glass Beatty's eyes are wide and amazed as she watches the woman pick up two sugar-tossed jellies with silver tongs and drop them into a small paper bag.

"One shilling and sixpence," she says, twisting the bag.

Fumbling in my pockets I count out the exact money, I drop my best low bow, take the bag and swing back out on to the street as if I bought jellies every day.

"Beatty?"

The pavement outside the shop's empty.

"Beatty?!"

Frantically I scan the people rushing through the market, and catch sight of a tall man with a glimpse of Beatty's red blanket just in front of him. Jamming the paper bag in my pocket I throw myself through the crowd to arrive by the side of the chair.

"Ah, Mr Wilde." It's Mr Katz. "I saw your sister shivering on the pavement, so I thought I would show her something more interesting."

"Oh!" I say. "I wondered where she'd gone."

Mr Katz does a deep bow. "So sorry if I alarmed you,"

"Thank you for looking after her," I say, holding out the paper bag to Beatty who lets out a gasp as she peers inside.

"Watch," says Mr Katz. "These people are very clever with their selling." He points to a man behind a small wooden stand and positions Beatty so that she has a ringside seat.

"Now, madam," says the man, turning towards a woman in a bloodstained apron. "What are life's greatest pests?"

"Ooh, my," says the woman, placing one raw hand on her hip, the other on her forehead. "You got me there. Seagulls? They're terrors, take lamb chops right off the stall, they do."

Everyone murmurs and nods. "Squirrels," calls someone else.

"Rats — rats everywhere."

"So rats, seagulls, squirrels — all of them fear me," the man cries, taking a small catapult from a sack and a felt ball from the bucket. "And this is why."

He holds up the catapult and takes aim. I don't see the felt ball fly but I do see the man on the other side of the square look around in amazement as the cap from his head leaps sideways and flies apparently unaided across the square.

The crowd laughs and we join in.

"You see the power unleashed, and imagine what a dried pea — yes, a dried pea, ladies and gentlemen — could do to vermin."

"Very good," mutters the meat woman.

"I think," says Beatty, "that it might be a waste of a good dried pea."

"Shh, child," hisses a woman with a basket of pigs' ears.

The meat woman glares at Beatty.

The showman presses a catapult into the meat

woman's hand. "Would the young lady like to demonstrate?"

The meat woman flutters her eyelashes and picks a felt ball from the bucket. Scanning the market, she looks for a target, fixing on a strolling seagull.

"Do you like marzipan?" Mr Katz asks Beatty.

Beatty flushes. "Yes – of course I do."

"Here." Mr Katz snaps a piece from a bar in his pocket and hands it to Beatty. She sticks it in her mouth and glows.

He hands me a piece half the size.

"Thank you," I say.

"Ladies and gentleman," says the showman. "Watch."

The meat woman plays the tension, obviously waiting until the crowd's grown. She pulls the leather back and fires, catching the seagull on the beak and sending it squawking into the air.

"Isn't that marvellous!" she cries. "What a wonderful thing!"

"Fine shot, ma'am," says the showman.

"Very good," says Mr Katz.

The crowd clap and rush forward to buy the catapults, and it suddenly occurs to me that something like a catapult might launch the flying machine. I wish I could ask Mr Chen.

"Perhaps I will buy one," says Mr Katz. "Here, boy, pay for me, will you?"

When I get back with the catapult and Mr Katz's change, he is bent over Beatty, telling her a joke, making her laugh. Her eyes shine and she takes another piece of marzipan.

The showman comes over to sell a catapult to Beatty.

"Sorry," I say, swinging the chair round so that we can get out of the crowd. "No money."

He scowls.

"Sorry, sir," yells Beatty over her shoulder. "Thanks for the show. Your friend you gave the thing to was a very good shot. I expect she's had a lot of practice."

But even as the people laugh we wriggle among them. Behind us I hear squeals and complaints but push on and on until we pop out the other side of the crowd with Mr Katz following.

Chapter 13

Mr Katz walks back with us across the square. He chatters to Beatty and asks me a few questions about what kind of work I did for Mr Chen.

"This and that, polishing, distilling, manufacturing."

"So he thought well of you? He trusted you?"

"I don't know – he used me quite a bit, most days."

"Ah. And what was he working on?"

It's on the tip of my tongue, but I let it slide and say, "Oh! Little machines for this and that, you know, rat traps, sundials. That kind of thing."

Mr Katz nods his head and smiles to himself.

Grandma shuffles off down to the kitchen as we return, and I stoke the little fire in the shop grate until the shop becomes almost snug.

Beatty sits next to it, playing with paper and folding birds nearly as good as the ones Mr Chen had.

"So when you are a stinking man, Athan, will you still visit us?"

"Yes, of course, but I won't be a stinking man."

The bell on the door rings and a woman comes in. I bow deeply and my eyes trace up from her delicate little feet. It's the sharp-faced woman from the auction. What's she doing here?

"Ribbon," she demands.

"For what purpose, madam?" I ask, pretending I've never seen her before.

"For my bonnet," she says, looking around the room, taking in the doors, the window, everything. She grabs at the bonnet balanced on her shoulders and swings it around.

It looks perfectly ribboned to me, but I glance at Beatty, whose finger creeps out of her scarf and points to a set of drawers under the counter. I don't work in the shop often enough to remember where everything is.

With a flourish, I pull the top drawer open, revealing row after row of neatly folded ribbons arranged in a rainbow. I set it three inches open, and pull the next one six inches open and the third, nine inches open, just as my pa did when I was little.

"Hmm," the woman says, pulling out one, then another, then a third, and taking each one to the window before discarding them on the floor. "What do you think? Boy?"

Beatty raises her eyebrows and clamps her hand over her mouth, but a snigger sneaks out. I tilt my head this way and that, giving the ribbons a good look. Beatty's right to laugh; I don't actually have a clue.

The woman looks over to Beatty by the fire. "Well, you're a very…" Words fail her. "Child," she says.

"Yes," says Beatty through her fingers. "I am a child."

"The yellow is very fresh," I say, dragging the woman's attention back to the ribbon. "And the orange."

"Only the mad wear orange, boy," says Grandma, appearing in the doorway, shortly followed by the smell of mothballs. She grins horridly at the woman.

"Oh!" says the woman, obviously shocked by the appearance of this witch from the basement. "Perhaps I'll take a little purple." She takes a lilac ribbon from the drawer and drops it on the counter top. "A yard will do." Suddenly she's in a hurry. Never did I think of Grandma as a guard dog, but perhaps in her horrible way, she is.

I measure out the ribbon against the brass yard on the counter, nip it neatly and drop it into a paper bag.

The woman throws a coin on the counter, grabs the ribbon and swings out of the shop.

"Ooh!" says Beatty. "What on earth did she really come in for?"

Polly's still out, and there's only Grandma asleep in the kitchen.

I go out to check on the hens. They've gone to roost, and I hang sacking over the front of their boxes, to keep at least the snow out, and slam the kitchen shutters closed.

Building up the kitchen stove, I put the kettle on and brew a pot of tea. I check the back door and the shutters again, thinking of Uncle and wondering why Polly isn't back yet.

"Are you afeared of the bogeyman?" asks Beatty, sipping at a cup.

"No – I'm not – but I'm afraid of foxes."

"Was that woman a fox?" asks Beatty.

"She might be either," I say, thinking of her with the scarred man, wandering around the auction, bidding against me.

"Is she to do with the thing you've got, the round

thing?"

I kneel down in front of Beatty. "You don't know anything about that, do you?" I say. "If anyone asks, you've never seen it, have you?"

Beatty shakes her head.

"Because it's not safe for you to know anything at all about it. Poll doesn't know, nor Ma – so you shouldn't either."

"But I always feel safe with you, Athan." A smile spreads over her little face. "Do you always feel safe with me?"

"Yes, Beatty, I do," I reply.

"Will you always look after me, Athan?"

"Yes, always," I say. "I promise."

From upstairs, the door knocker echoes through the house. We run up together, her on my hip, and peer out into the gloom.

It's not Poll, it's Tod.

"Need your help, Athan," he says. "Round at Mr Katz's place. We're knocking down a wall – bit heavy with just the two of us. He thought you might help?"

"Thing is, Tod," I say. "Poll's out and I don't want to leave Beatty on her own in the house with Grandma."

"I'll be all right, Athan," says Beatty. "You go and earn some money and gaze at Mary. I've got a sugar mouse to suck."

I carry her down to the kitchen and settle her by the range. Grandma's there, stirring something.

She glances up at me. "I'll keep an eye on the fairy child, don't you worry, boy."

For a moment I stand in the doorway, not sure if I should leave Beatty there, but she waves me away, picks up a scrap of newspaper and begins to fold a new bird.

I follow Tod over the packed snow to New King Street. Although I'm wearing my new jacket and a muffler and my old leather boots, I'm still cold. The ice glitters like diamonds where there are house lights, and our feet crack through the top layer of snow into the dung underneath.

In the distance something crashes.

"Snow's brought down a roof, I'll guess," Tod says, skidding on the ice.

I think about the kite up there on the church tower, sagging with snow. "Do you think we could get the machine up into your loft?"

"Tonight?"

"We should move it as soon as we can," I say.

Tod pulls his jacket closer around his ears. "You're right. After work?"

The tiny pox-scarred woman I saw the first time is at

Mr Katz's house. She opens the door but disappears back down to the kitchen without saying a word.

We stumble down the narrow stairs to what ought to be a kitchen, steam filled and well lit.

Mary appears in the doorway opposite, her sleeves rolled up, a length of brass tubing in her arms.

"Hello, Athan," she says.

I don't know why I blush, I just do.

Mary giggles and runs up the stairs.

"*Wilkommen*, welcome, my good friend." Mr Katz, now in shirtsleeves and a waistcoat, comes in through the garden door. As he does so, the steam floats out and the icy air rushes in to replace it. "How splendid. One minute and I'll be back." He grabs a hammer and dashes up the stairs.

"Why's he knocking down a wall?" I ask, closing the door.

Tod takes off his jacket. "He wants to build a huge telescope, see further into the heavens than anyone's ever seen before. Mary's helping him build it – but the new one needs a space in the garden; there's no room without knocking down the wall. If you go outside, you can take a look."

"D'you mean you've looked at the stars close up and you didn't tell me?" I give Tod a shove. He staggers and shoves me back.

"I didn't see anything – it wobbled about and my eye hurt staring up at the black. But she spends hours out there. She's lookin' for comets." Tod rubs his head. "Or meteors, or somethin'."

"Who?"

"His sister, Caroline." He nods over his shoulder towards the back door.

"Go on, she won't bite ... much."

After the steam of the workshop, the outside air seems ferociously cold. I glance up. The sky glitters with stars and the moon hangs clear and impossibly clear.

In the middle of the garden, a long wooden box points at the sky. I can't see Caroline until a black bundle on the ground shuffles and a pale oval face appears.

"You wish?" she asks me, and points at the wooden barrel. "Is good moon. Clear tonight, the sky?"

I kneel down on the freezing snow, the cold soaking right through my breeches, and lay my head down on the wet ground so that I can get near the eyepiece. At first I can't work out which eye I need to close, then I gaze into blackness before the end of the telescope explodes with silver light.

I start. I stare.

I'm amazed. This is the moon but it's huge and pale, and as I gaze I see more lines and spots until it becomes like a mad embroidery of silver threads criss-crossing the circle of the lens.

I stare until my eyes hurt.

So bold in the blackness.

So silver.

So cold.

I pull myself away so that I can look up at the sky without the tube. The moon's just a pale white line in the sky now. Something far away and nothing to me. For a moment back then it seemed that I could touch it, understand its secrets. Fly to it.

I'm about to have another look when Mr Katz and Tod appear beside me.

"Right, boys, let us move this little wall out of the way. Ready?"

Mr Katz doesn't offer me work, but he does tip me a shilling. I slip the coin into my boot and wait for Tod on the doorstep.

It's cold and the gutters burn our fingers but we totter over the roof of the little chapel and into the church tower. The kite, sagging with snow, looks tattered and bedraggled. We'd put it up here to launch it but, as Mr Chen said, we'd need a gale from the right direction, and we don't have the house as a workshop any more. There's just no point in leaving it there.

"Is it still all right?" asks Tod.

I check the bamboo structure underneath. It weighs nothing, but it's so strong it hasn't even bent beneath the snowfall. "I reckon so," I say. "I think we should drag it over to Mr Chen's house, and then on down the row until the buildings get lower."

We shake the snow from the wings and I undo the ropes at the front of the kite so that the whole thing folds like an umbrella. Some of the fabric comes off, but we wrap it around and use the ropes to truss it all together.

Tod scrambles across to Mr Chen's roof and I feed the bundle over to him.

"Shhh," says Tod, and I look down to see a crack of light around the trapdoor below our feet. Then someone tries to open it.

I'd forgotten that Mrs Love has let Mr Chen's house again already.

My weight is on the trap, so I lean a little and the person below gives up, presumably imagining the snow thicker and heavier than it is.

We stand waiting as the square light fades, listening for footsteps. A candle makes its way down the house, reflecting off the wall all the way down until I see it shining into the back yard.

"They're in the kitchen," I say. "Quick, let's get this done."

It's heavy, and cold, and soggy, but between us, dragging and pushing, we manage to get it over the high roofs until we're able to drop down the lower ones. It's all going really well until Tod moves too far ahead and loses his balance.

He drops the kite and I watch his arms windmill. Then his whole body starts to tip.

"Tod, no!"

And he vanishes.

I drop the kite and lean over the side of the roof.

"Tod?"

"Athan," he calls from the darkness. There's a sloshing sound.

"Where are you?"

"In the horse trough."

"Are you all right?"

"Cold," he says in answer, and I hear the shiver in his voice. "And stuck in this yard."

"There's a pipe over the other side." I point.

Someone throws open a window.

"What's that racket? Someone there?"

A dog begins to bark and another dog joins in.

I hear Tod's feet against the pipe as he clambers up

and I move around the roofs until I can reach down and give him a hand.

"Don't tell Da," he says, staggering to his feet on the roof.

"Don't tell Ma," I say.

We start again, slipping and skidding all the way, skinning fingers in the cold, pinching thumbs and swearing. Once we're on the ground, we have to scuttle through the streets, lugging the folded kite, dodging sedan chairs and carriages until we reach the timber yard where we take it around the side, tiptoeing over the rotten wharf until we're right below Tod's loft built high above the river above the coffin shop and timber store.

Tod shins up the back and drops a rope to me. I tie it around the tip of the kite and raise my hand. He pulls, and steadily the whole thing rises up the back of the building. Racing up the gutter I help him get it up the last few feet, pushing it away from the sides and then pulling it up.

"One more heave," he says.

Together, we dig in our heels and drag, and apart from a distant sound of ripping, the kite glides obediently on to the flat roof.

"Well," says Tod, crumpling to the ground and letting go of the rope.

"Yes," I say. Taking off my jacket and muffler and letting out the heat.

"We've got it," he says. "Safe and sound."

"We have," I say. "All we have to do is bring everything else up here. Fire her up and think of a way to launch her," I say, remembering the showman and his felt balls. "Maybe we build a giant catapult."

"As easy as that," says Tod, peeling off his wet breeches.

"Yes," I say, pushing all thoughts of the scarred stranger and the sharp-faced woman to the side. "As easy as that."

Chapter 14

I'm thinking about catapults and moons and flight when I step into our shop. The door's open and I stop to listen. A kind of wailing and grumbling rises up the kitchen stairs. I pull down the blinds and follow the sounds.

It takes me a moment to work out what's happening. In the centre of the room, Columbine Good is crouching between Beatty and the stove. On the floor is a jug of steaming yellow paste, and Columbine's dipping lengths of bandage into it, then prodding them with a wooden spoon before hooking them out and draping them across Beatty's legs.

"Do you think it's already working?" Grandma asks. She stands behind Columbine, her brown-spotted hands on her hips.

"What's she doing?" I ask.

"Curing the fairy child – driving out the devils in her legs. Then we can swap her for the real Beatty. Send the changeling back." Grandma moves between me and Columbine, who speeds up the wrapping.

"Get off her. She's not a changeling – she's my sister." I try to push Columbine away, but Grandma slaps me across my neck with the carpet beater.

"Ow!" I push at Grandma, but she picks up a stool and jabs at me with the legs, driving it between me and Beatty. "The fairies are very clever, boy, they leave us with their cripple and take our strong baby to work as their slave." She's good with the stool, using it like a sword. "Now, you let us get on with it."

"No! This isn't right – get off her!" I demand, just as Grandma swipes the stool up under my chin, sending me backwards across the kitchen.

"Black mustard, iron filings and chillis," answers Columbine. "S'worked afore, no reason to think it won't. And the digitalis, she must drink the digitalis."

Digitalis, digitalis, what's digitalis? I know I've heard of it. Shaking my head I get to my feet.

"It stings," says Beatty. Her face is red from tears.

"Bound to," Columbine says. "But it'll be worth it to send you home. Mark my words."

"Take them off," I say, finally getting a grip on the legs of the stool and shoving it and Grandma to one side. Leaning over, I grab at Columbine's hands, trying to undo the knots holding the strips to Beatty's feeble legs. Columbine stands back and I scrabble at the bandages. She passes Beatty a cup of something green. Beatty sips it and gags.

"Don't drink it," I shout, and I remember what it is. "They're poisoning you. It's foxgloves."

Beatty leaves the cup on the side, but her legs twitch even as I yank at the swaddling. It's burning my hands. The women stand back, waiting.

"Get water, you silly old bat," I say.

"Work's done, boy," Grandma barks. "Your meddling won't make any difference. Any minute now the fairies'll come down and whisk this little devil away — along with all our bad fortune."

"But it burns, Grandma, it hurts. Athan, make it stop."

Grandma leans back against the stove, watching her handiwork. Watching Beatty squirm. "That's right, child, we'll burn you out, so hold your tongue. Salvation won't be far away," she says. "Then the imps as make you sick'll be burned right out, and the fairies'll want you back. That's right, isn't it?"

Tears race down Beatty's face, her cheeks aflame.

"Just a little while longer," says Columbine. "Drive out the demons, won't we. Those nasty demons that stops you walking and suchlike." She starts to sing.

"There was thirteen imps all dancing in chains,
She upped with her shoes and beat out their brains."

The knots are harder and harder to undo, my hands become slick with the burning mustard mixture and I struggle as Columbine laughs and subsides in a mustardy heap on the floor. She's quite mad now.

I manage to free one leg. "If you keep that up it won't work, you idiot!" shouts Grandma, yanking my hair.

"It isn't going to work anyway," I yell back.

"Water, Athan, water," Beatty shouts, dabbing the stuff from her knees with her pinny.

Suddenly Polly's on the stairs. "What's going on?" she asks.

Columbine sits at Beatty's feet, rocking and singing to herself. Grandma thrashes my back with the carpet beater.

"You cursed boy, you crack-brained nazzard." She hits me again.

"Oh, Beatty, what have the old fools done to you?!"

Polly runs to fetch cloths to help wipe off the muck.

"Oh, Poll – I think they've really hurt her." I pour the lukewarm water from the kettle over Beatty's shaking legs and my own burning hands but the poultice still won't come off.

Polly drags at Columbine, who sits limp on the flagstones, still singing. "Come on, you're not wanted," says Polly, hooking her hands under the old woman's arms and pulling. "Look what you've done to Beatty, you old bat," she shouts at Grandma.

"No more than she deserves," says Grandma, picking up some of the heap of yellow bandage on the floor and trying to drape it over Beatty's leg. "Mark my words, she's not of this Earth."

"Ooh, Athan, it's getting worse," sobs Beatty.

In all the fuss, I don't hear her coming in, but suddenly there's Ma, dressed up to the nines.

"Goodness My Lord, what is going on? Athan? Poll?"

Grandma freezes but Columbine goes on singing. The kitchen's spotted with yellow, and more yellow oozes from the bandage to snake around Beatty's chair. She wails and sobs and dabs at her skin.

"It hurts, Ma, it's like fire," she cries.

"Oh, my poor love!" Ma comes over and presses Beatty's head to her chest.

"What's all the fuss about?" says a soft northern voice.

I turn and see the scarred man from the inn standing there in our kitchen, dressed like a lord.

My heart stops. What's he doing here?

"Whatever must you think of us?" says Ma, patting her ringlets. "Athan, let me introduce you. This is Colonel Blade."

Chapter 15

"How nice to meet you again. Athan, isn't it?" The man holds out his hand.

His cold eyes fix on mine and I choke on a greeting.

First the sharp-faced woman and now him. Both of them in our house on the same day.

"Help me get these things in the fire." Polly rescues me and I stuff the oily bandages into the range while she wipes the last of the burning mustard from Beatty's legs. Together we bundle Columbine up the stairs and tip her out into the road. Sneaking a glance at the Colonel as we go, I notice that he's standing very close to Ma, touching her arm. Intimate, as if they've known each other forever.

"Is that her fancy man?" I ask Polly when we're standing in the shop together.

"Yes," Polly smiles. "Never thought she'd get one." And she rushes back down the stairs to the kitchen.

Following her, I scoop up Beatty and carry her upstairs to the drawing room only to find Ma settling the Colonel into a seat in front of our fire and giving him a cup of our tea. She wobbles on to the chaise longue, giggling and talking in a silly high voice. He's wearing full finery and talking like a gentleman, with only a touch of coal in his speech and you could mistake him for the real thing.

Dazed, I sit on a footstool, melting snow on my burning palms as Ma prattles on about Uncle. All the time the Colonel lies back in our chair as if it was his own. His black boots gleam in the firelight, his fingers play on the arm of the chair. Our chair.

I've left Beatty on the other side of the room wrapped in her blanket, her burned legs resting in a pail full of snow.

So all that stuff in the inn. It was for real. He really does know.

If I could, I'd lift my entire family up and take them away, hide them somewhere a long way from this man. But instead I find him here at the heart of us and for almost the first time in my life, I can't think what to do.

"So tell me about this Mr Chen then." The Colonel watches me as he speaks. He picks up a piece of our coal and throws it on our fire.

"Oh, he was very nice, a very polite man, charming," Ma babbles.

"A heathen," shouts Grandma from her armchair. "A disciple of Mephistopheles."

"Shush, Mother," says Ma, a flash of real anger in her face. "You stay quiet. You've done enough damage today." She turns back to the Colonel, all smiles. "He was a Natural Philosopher you know."

"Was he?" says the Colonel, as if he didn't care. I watch him brush a flake of ash from the arm of the chair.

"Oh yes, he made black powder and all sorts in his kitchen – always boiling things up."

"And blowing things up!" snorts Grandma. "Blew up the henhouse in October – feathers all over the shop – hens all to pieces. Never a word of sorry from him, just laughed and did it again."

"He paid for new hens and brought us a box of cherries, Grandma," says Polly, offering more tea.

I watch them talking, and I watch him listen. His eyes dance about, not missing a thing. His gaze rests on the things on the walls: framed maps, pictures. When he's checked all of these he gets up and wanders about, peering under the couch and the sofa. No one else seems to notice, but he's looking for something.

And I know what it is.

I force myself not to look towards the clock where I hid Mr Chen's sphere. His cold blue eyes are on mine, a smile moving over his lips. So I study the tobacco box on the mantelpiece, and then Uncle's fiddle case. Perhaps if I gaze hard enough at them, he'd think Mr Chen's secret's hidden there.

"Ma, I think I'm gonna be ill, Ma." Beatty's voice sounds odd. "Athan, take me to bed."

She's pale as death.

I go over to her, and on the way I push the violin case under the sofa. Perhaps I'm overdoing it, but it's worth a try. I pick up Beatty. "D'you want a bit of fresh air?"

"I want to go to bed, Athan."

I carry her upstairs and lay her down. She grabs her rag doll and holds it close.

"I didn't say nothing about the ball, Athan."

"No, you didn't." I smile at her pale face peeking round the doll's dress. "Thank you, Beatty."

"You don't like him, do you, Athan?"

I shake my head. "I don't trust him."

"And what about the ribbon lady?"

"I think she's his friend. I don't trust either of them."

"Why?" she asks, then screws up her face in pain.

"Does it still hurt?" I ask.

"It burns like hellfire, Athan. Is it a punishment for being sickly, for being a fairy baby?"

"Course not," I say, and take hold of her hand. "It's just two daft old women." I take the candle and look at her legs. The skin's lifted, like it does on a baked apple, and beneath is angry shining flesh. It doesn't look right and I begin to worry.

"This woun' a happened if Pappy was still here – he'd not have let them near me."

"Maybe," I say. Although it was when Beatty was born that our father moved out and Grandma moved in, almost to the day. I remember Grandma stamping up the road with her boxes and moving into Polly's room as if she owned it. Holding Beatty to her chest Ma had stood on the stairs her face all tear-stained, and collapsed.

It all started to go wrong that day.

I can't help it. When I get back to the sitting room, I glance up at the clock. The sphere's still there. I sneak a look at the Colonel, his eyes glistening in the lamplight. It flickers over his scars and picks out the gold of his tooth.

Ma leaves the room to check on Beatty.

I sit with Polly and the Colonel in the drawing room. The clock ticks loudly.

A carriage rumbles down the street outside.

Grandma clears her throat and falls back to snoring.

The hair on the back of my neck prickles upright and although the room's stuffy, I shiver.

Ma comes back and settles herself by the fire, opposite the Colonel, like they make a pair.

"What will you do tomorrow, sir?" asks Polly of the Colonel.

He shakes his head idly and gazes up at the clock.

I hold my breath.

"The Baths; perhaps a soiree? There's a game started at the assembly rooms." He stares at me. "It might amuse me. Play a few cards." He's talking like a diamond but I know he's a piece of coal.

"Oh!" Polly mutters.

The Colonel's hands drum on the arm of the chair. He picks up a stick from the hearth and shreds it between his fingers, burning one strand at a time.

"Anything in the paper, Poll?" I ask, filling the silence.

"A man who says he can turn a wild dog into a calm dog by swapping over their blood, that's on at the theatre — *Cox's Mechanical Marvels,* up from London. Oh!" Polly goes white and flaps her hand at the paper. *"Horrible Murder. This morning, Haddock the auctioneer was found viciously harmed unto death. His damaged corpse was left hanging from Mr Wood's new crescent. His tongue. . .* Oh! I can't read that out," she winces. *"The town hall is mystified and asks for witnesses to come forward.* Oh goodness — poor Mr Haddock. Poor Mrs Haddock!"

I keep my face stony still.

Polly goes on reading. "It says here, 'His wife and son'. . . I didn't know he had a son — poor little thing." Polly sighs and hands the paper to Ma.

"My!" The Colonel raises an eyebrow. "That sounds most unpleasant — who was this Haddock then?"

Polly explains about the Haddock family, but I don't really hear what she says.

Haddock and Uncle, *and* Mr Chen?

I look up at the Colonel.

There he is, sitting in our drawing room, with me, and the sphere, and my sister. Outside in the yard all the pieces of the flying machine.

He isn't listening to Polly. He's laughing, sharing a joke with himself, and his eyes are on mine, and stare back for the longest time, until, in the end, smiling, he looks away.

Slipping down into the basement, I open the back door and hide in the yard, talking to the hens. I listen to their comforting little cheeps. The squeaks and pecks, and feather rustling. I pick up Big Hen. She lies passive and half sleeping against my belly, warm and comforting. Under the feathers she's lean and bony, but she's stronger than she feels; she's escaped firebombs and foxes and laid an egg every day for three years.

"What's he doing here then?" I ask her.

She answers by gently pecking at my wrist and I slip her back into the topmost port box.

A horrible image of Colonel Blade sneaking through Mr Chen's house, bloody dagger in hand, fills my head and I have to calm myself by checking up on all the pieces of the machine, pulling the oil cloth tight over them, keeping them safe.

Shivering, not just from the cold, I wait outside in gently falling snow until I'm sure he's gone and decide that when the house is quiet I'll get the handcart out and take everything I can down to Tod's. Plans and all.

Back in the kitchen, I damp down the stove and duck upstairs to the shop to pull down the shutters and bolt the door. Turning to run back to the warmth of the parlour I see him, standing in the shadows of the shop. His hand on the shoulder of a mannequin, as if he owned the place.

"Ah," he says. His mouth opens blackly. "I wondered where you'd got to." His voice is soft and black. "I've been talking with your ma, but time to lay me head down now, get a bit of sleep. I've got what I came for. I know what I'm doing next. Time to take stock." He wanders idly to the door.

"Oh," I say, keeping my back to the basement stairs.

"Delicate little flower, in't she, your sister? Glad no harm's come." He speaks almost gently.

I nod.

"You'd better watch out for her, being her older brother and that." His voice is barely above a whisper.

I stay silent.

"Night night, sleep tight, don't let the bogeyman bite." He laughs, pulls back the bolts and heads off into the snow.

I run to check but the sphere's still hidden behind the clock. He hasn't taken it.

Chapter 16

Polly and I sit on either side of Beatty's bed, far into the night.

"Have you found work?" Polly whispers.

I shake my head. "No, but I will."

"She's sending Beatty away." The words are very quiet in the dark room, and I look at Polly to see if she really said it.

Her eyes are damp. "The Colonel says he can take Beatty to a charity hospital in London where they can look after her and cure her legs."

"But, Poll, she can't!"

"I don't see how we can stop it. We—" Polly goes

quiet.

Ma stands in the doorway, her face stretched into a wide smile. "I'll take over now, Poll. You get some sleep." But I can see she's been crying.

We sit on either side of Beatty's bed until the city goes silent.

"She's peaceful now," whispers Ma. "But I'll stay till light."

I lean back on my chair and watch them.

Hen and chick.

"What a day!" She smiles. "What a lovely man. Paid the doctor's bill for your uncle, no questions asked."

"Why?"

"Because he's a nice man." Ma strokes Beatty's cheek. "He can change all our lives, a man like that."

I say nothing.

"Such a fine upstanding man. Broad shouldered. Kind. I never would have thought—"

I have to say something.

"Ma, you don't know anything about him."

"I do. He's told me lots. All very impressive."

"I..." I can't say it. "You can't send Beatty away. It's not right."

She looks up at me, her face red and wet. "I don't want to, boy, but I don't have a choice. This'll give Beatty the chance of a better life."

"Beatty's almost never been out of the house. You can't send her to live in some hospital." I try to sound calm. "She'll be miserable."

I imagine Beatty carted off in a wagon, the Colonel smiling alongside her.

"You only met him this morning."

"He's a bit rough about the edges, I grant you, but solid underneath." She picks a curl from Beatty's forehead and pushes it to the side. "He'll look after her."

"Ma, listen. You can't trust him! You don't know him!"

"I do – I can. You'll work for the nightmen and Beatty'll be safe in a hospital, it's the way—"

"Ma! Stop! Think what you're doing to the family."

"Off you go, boy – go to sleep now."

She waves me away and I rise from the bedside.

"Don't trust him – he's—"

But she pushes me out through the door and leaves me standing on the landing in the dark.

Chapter 17

In the morning, before the light's up properly, I go up to check on Beatty. She's asleep. Pale on her pillow, her legs uncovered. Raw.

I run into Grandma on the stairs, carrying her chamber pot down to the yard.

"Evil witch," I mutter.

"What's that?" she says, her hand cupped against her ear.

"Nothing, Grandma," I say, whipping past her to the shop, where I throw up the blinds and light the lanterns with a flint.

I kindle a fire in the grate and turn the sign so that

people know we're open.

Mr Katz is our first customer and I welcome him in, offering him coffee and stale cake and hollering for Polly to measure him for a waistcoat.

"And how are you, young Mr Wilde? Have you found work yet?" he says, taking off his jacket and handing it to me. I drape it over the back of a chair.

"No, sir, I haven't, but I've hopes."

"I may have a little more for you in a day or so. Let me think on it."

"Light the range, Athan." Polly sends me downstairs while she gets busy with a tape measure.

I slip down to the kitchen and shake the stove to life, rattling the ashes out from last night. And then I go out to check on the hens.

I know something's wrong.

The yard's too quiet. Too still.

I stop outside the kitchen door and listen.

There is no sound at all from the makeshift henhouse.

I look down at the snow. No fox prints. No cat prints.

No blood.

But there are boot prints.

Slowly, I lift the flap on the front of the wine boxes and reach inside.

Their bodies are still warm. Eyes open.

Necks broken.

All eight hens, together.

Dead.

I carry the brass engine down to Tod's.

"You mean he sneaked in your yard and wrung their necks?"

"Yup," I say, resting the engine on the floor of the loft.

A shadow crosses Tod's face.

"I know," I say, biting back the tears.

"And you left the house?"

I try to sound as if I'm not worried. "Ma and Poll are there this morning. Mr Katz was upstairs having a fitting. They're safe, for now," I say, wishing I believed myself.

"God, Athan – don't you think you should be careful?"

"I am being careful!" I snap.

"But he knows, doesn't he?" says Tod, rubbing a cloth over the brass.

I shake my head. "I think he knows there are plans. I think that's what he's looking for – but he's not a scientist, he's just a soldier. He might be able to kill a man, but he doesn't know what the flying machine looks like."

"Oh." Tod looks at the tangle of sticks and silk and the engine. "That's all right then," he says, half grinning.

I walk back, and with every step my anger grows.

My beautiful hens.

My precious hens.

I'm punching walls by the time I get back but Polly heads me off. "Take this up to Alfred Street, will you, Athan?" She hands me a parcel.

"If I do, will you stay here, Poll?" I ask.

"Yes – why?"

"I don't want to leave Beatty or Ma on their own."

She looks at me. "Because?"

"Just because, and can you dress me neatly – do my hair in a plait?"

"Of course, why?"

"So that I can get work," I lie.

We do it in Beatty's room. My new jacket, my father's shoes, a waistcoat meant for another man, the breeches – cleaned – new stockings and a cravat.

Polly pins a brooch at my neck. "Keep still. I can't help you if you keep bobbing about."

"You look like a prince, Athan. If I kiss you, will I have new legs?" Beatty asks.

"Maybe," I answer.

"Shh now," mutters Polly. "Don't give her hopes." She stuffs something clammy and itchy on to my scalp, then wrenches it off and shakes powder all over it. She jams it back on my head.

"I'm not wearing that!" I pull the mangy second-hand wig off my head. "Just do me a queue, Poll – go on," I say.

"I still think you'll need the wig," she says, wrenching my hair back to plait it.

Beatty puts down the bird she's folding, crosses her eyes and sticks out her tongue. "Where you going dressed like a butterfly?" she asks.

"The assembly rooms, where all the people go to dance and that."

"Can I come?" she says.

"Not this time, little bird," I say, and I kiss her on the top of her head. "I'm trying to find a job. I'll be back before bedtime."

"Promise?" asks Beatty.

"Promise," I say. "Cross my heart and hope to die."

Chapter 18

I've left home without much of a plan.

Except that right now I want to break his neck.

I drop off the parcel and I'm approaching the assembly rooms when I hear her.

"Athan." I turn. "You look smart." It's Mary, from Mr Katz's. The blush rises from my neck to my nose and for a moment all I do is stand there with my mouth hanging open.

"Yes," I say in the end. And then I ask, "What are you doing here?"

"Oh, Mr Katz left his fiddle bow behind last night, I've come to look for it — you can help. Unless you're doing something else?"

"Looking for a job." I smile. Mary looks confused, and I see that she takes a moment to work out what I've said.

"Oh," she nods. "Good luck. Watch out though, there are some who never pay their bills. You don't want to find yourself working for them."

I follow her through the doors. We're noticed but ignored. She marches up to a man in a full frogged suit, busting with buttons and embroidery. "Mr Katz's bow, left here last night – where might I find it? And have you got any jobs going for him?" She tilts her head in my direction. I puff out my chest and point my toes and generally look as dandy as I can.

The man indicates a little door to the side of the stairs. "Try the cupboard." He stares at me, weighing me up as if I was a horse. "Perhaps," he says, before screwing his face into a cascade of welcoming smiles and turning towards an overblown woman and her giggling daughter gliding across the tiles. "Welcome, ladies, welcome." He glances back at me. "Ask me again in a while. If my doorman doesn't turn up in the next ten minutes, you can have his job."

Cheered, I arrange to meet Mary in half an hour and enter the main rooms.

I've been here before, but always when it was empty

of visitors. Pa took me when he reupholstered the chairs. I notice that they're still here, dusty and a little faded, but still recognisably the same. Around them, the place is busting with skirts, and shining buttons, and people with crutches. Swarms rush this way and that, clanking tea cups and showing off their fancy clothes.

I look around for the Colonel.

I can't roll up my sleeves and punch him here, but perhaps I can arrange to meet him, and I can jump him outside. But for the time being I need to look like someone wanting work or I'll get thrown out.

An elderly couple are standing alone on one side of the room and the woman is struggling to hold a walking stick, a bag, and a cup and saucer. I swoop up alongside them. "Can I help?" I say.

"Oh, yes, if you'd just take this," says the woman, rattling the cup at me. I grab it and her elbow, and help her to a chair.

"Athan Wilde at your service," I say, smiling.

The man slips me a penny and turns his back, dismissing me.

Walking away, I turn the penny in my pocket and try to think of a better way of loitering in here — when I spot the Colonel. He's standing with his back to me in the main hallway talking to someone. I hide behind a pillar to eavesdrop.

"Colonel Blade, dear fellow, join us in a game?" says a voice. "Stakes are high, we've a rich idiot to fleece, join me for the kill?" It's a posh voice. I poke my head around to see the Colonel swept down the hall and into an eight-sided room by a man with shining shoes and a very well-tailored jacket.

He's a real gent and he makes Blade look tatty.

I follow.

The room's set out with card tables and Blade sits down at one with his back to me. There are four fireplaces, four mirrors and some portraits of fat men in waistcoats. The ceiling's murky and coated with candle soot, but I think it's one of those grand ones with pictures and lumpy plaster.

I peer at myself in the mirror and see that my hair, normally dark, looks like I've seen a ghost, thanks to Polly's talcum powder. I wander over to a fireplace and brush as much powder into the fire as I can. It burns with a pop, so that the people in the room turn round to see what's caused the noise.

I pretend it has nothing to do with me.

I turn my back on Blade, keeping my eyes on him using the mirror that hangs over the fireplace. He never takes his eyes from the table, never moves out into the shadows.

I want to listen to their conversation but there's no cover. Perhaps I could try earwigging from the hallway and I head towards the doorway as calmly as I can but a man with a tray of drinks trips on the step and blunders into me.

"Oh my goodness. Oh I'm so terribly sorry," hoots the man who has poured hot dark chocolate down my sleeve. "Oh damn – blast."

Now everyone's staring at us. Including Blade.

"Let's mop you down," says a large woman sailing in our direction, brandishing a cloth.

"Lad." Blade's suddenly at my elbow, smiling. "How pleasant to see you. A little accident with your nice coat?" He tugs at me. "We'll sort him out," he says to the woman as he pulls me from the crowd. "Have a drink." He pats me on the back.

I follow, wondering if I could bring him down now.

He steers me over to a table. He presses a cup into my hand and dabs at my jacket with a grubby hanky. Unsure of what to do I down the cup. It's like tea, only not.

A second later, another cup appears in my hand. I empty it in one gulp. It's nice and sweet, and I feel ready and bold. I laugh.

My mouth opens. "Colonel – I want you to, I want to tell you to—"

Blade lets go of my shoulders and sits down. "No need to talk now. Watch the game, lad." He's got a smile on his face. "Don't take your eyes from the game."

Somehow I feel as if I'm watching myself from the outside. Surely these heavy arms don't belong to me – or these useless legs? The useless legs fold and I sink to a chair. Cards come and go in front of me; piles of money go back and forth across the table.

Someone makes a joke, and I look up at my neighbours. The other men all wear uniform, but they're not smart. One of them's missing a finger, the stump's bound with a dirty bandage; another's unshaven, the third's got no teeth. Where's the man in the expensive clothes?

I drink another cup of the thick sweet tea.

The Colonel writes something on a piece of paper and gives it to the most toothless one, who leaves the table and disappears into the crowds. I try to follow, but my legs have gone soft.

"We'll play a round, no stakes. Or tell you what, lad, I'll lend you a guinea. Use it, see if it gives you any luck." They all laugh. This time their eyes seem darker, their mouths wider.

Hearts, clubs, diamonds, clubs, diamonds ... pretty pictures in my hand.

I gulp down tea. The stump-fingered one fills my cup from a teapot. I drink that too. I'm thirsty; why am I so thirsty? And the room seems very full and very noisy.

"Why am I here? I can't remember why I'm here."

"Don't know, lad," says the Colonel.

I begin to feel very hot. My cheeks are burning and my cravat's digging into my neck so I pull at the pin until the brooch gives up and falls out. The brooch feels cold and heavy in my hand, as if it disapproves of me.

It takes me two goes to get it in my pocket.

Somewhere I must have some feet. There's the floor, wooden, jagged, going in all directions like my head. Experimentally I see if the foot I can see is mine. It's at an odd angle, and it moves, but not how I expect. If I walk now, the floor will come too. If I stand, perhaps the floor will come to meet me. I try to stand but my head feels so heavy, it tries to dive all on its own.

"Carry him ... lift ... no one'll notice..." My legs slide over the floor. Someone grabs me under my arms and pulls. Something's happened to me. I've got no strength.

"Shocking at this time in the afternoon. I shall have to complain." A high voice rings in my ears, a woman sweeps past us, trailing sickly perfume.

"So sorry," I mutter.

"Try walking, lad. Try using your legs." The Colonel's on my left.

"Z'bones! Mordecai, he's heavy."

Who's Mordecai?

"Excuse us, miss."

My feet get caught in a dress.

"Don't come back for that job, boy – I don't employ drinkers," the man in the suit barks at me as we pass him.

I try to say, "I don't drink," but we don't stop for long enough for me to meet his eye and instead my useless legs catch in something that rustles. It lets out a squawk and the Colonel's arms get me outside. The rush of cold air hits me and for a moment I know where I am. Outside the assembly rooms.

I make an attempt to run but my legs fold and I sag back into his grasp.

"Why not do it now?" one of the soldiers asks.

"Not yet." Coins change hands and the Colonel mutters something about waiting for someone.

"If he spews here in front of our customers, it'll cost you twenty shillings," shouts the man from the doorway as a carriage pulls to a halt. I look up at him and vomit on his shoes.

Somebody in a yellow dress opens the door from inside and the Colonel shoves me up the little steps.

Something yelps as I climb in.

A dog.

I slump to one side, my face pressed against the glass. Blade says something to the driver then clambers up, wedging himself next to me.

"Dear God, what a smell." From the shadows comes a woman's voice, and a hand that flaps a white handkerchief.

"Open the window then," says Blade. "It's him and his vomit, they go t'gether."

We begin to move and the carriage groans over the cobbles.

The world spins back and forth so I close my eyes, but it just moves faster.

Something rustles on the seat opposite me. I prise my eyes open to look. It's the dog, clambering on to the seat. It growls at me and I nearly throw up again.

"Hold on to it, lad — have a sip on this." The Colonel passes me a silver flask. I put it to my lips and a burning stream of something pours down my throat. I cough and nearly retch, and sink against the side of the coach.

Perhaps I sleep, perhaps I stay awake, but I know he talks to me, talks in his soft coal town voice. And she stays quiet, her powdered face a white oval in the darkness, the man beside her no more than a square of handkerchief. They all ask questions, but I don't think I answer them, I don't think I can do or I'll be sick.

"What did you find at the old man's 'ouse?"

"Nothin'."

"Was there owt there?"

"No."

"Are you and your uncle th'only ones who went there?"

"Going to be sick."

I think we go round by the river then. I sleep, but when I wake the world's still going round.

"What was he working on?"

I don't answer. I'm sure I never say anything. "Was it a flying machine?" asks the woman. "Actually, we know it was a flying machine so there's no need not to tell us."

I don't answer.

"You see, he told us quite a lot, that last evening," says the woman. "It was a long night. A bloody night."

"Aye," says the Colonel, a grin creeping across his mouth. "There were plenty of blood."

The carriage lurches, and all the cups of tea that haven't already left me lurch too. "He lived a long time, that old man," she says almost regretfully.

"He cared about you," says the Colonel.

"He did," the woman says.

"Called out for you, he did," says the Colonel.

"Touching," says the woman.

"It was," agrees the Colonel.

"It's nice to see a soul caring about another soul. Shame we didn't get to you first. He'd have done anything for you."

"What's your greatest fear, boy?"

I don't answer.

At least, I don't think I do.

What seems like hours later, the Colonel asks, "Where d'you keep your secrets, lad?"

"Down my breeches." I laugh at that one.

"Is it under the bed, lad? Is there something special under your bed?"

"What? My thunder mug?" I giggle. I can't stop.

He smiles; he goes on smiling at me, his heavy hand resting on my knee. His head shakes up and down in the carriage, like a puppet.

I think I'm asleep when the woman says, "I think you need to understand, Athan, that there's a great deal at stake here. Not just a little misplaced loyalty – we need to know what you know – and we will. Whether or not you want to tell us."

I know we stay in that carriage for a long time, rattling over the streets, passing door after door, the snow on the pavements, the door again, the pavements, the voices all going on and on, on and on, on and on.

"He's asleep," says Blade.

"We're going to have to get it somehow," says the woman.

We swing right.

"Do you think he knows much?" she asks.

"Enough," says Blade. "More than anyone else."

"How are we going to find out?"

We swing left. There's a really long silence. I might even fall asleep.

"I know. I know exactly how to get it," says the Colonel with a smile in his voice.

And I never say anything, I don't think.

I really don't.

Chapter 19

I dream of foxes nipping the necks of hens. Hens wearing dresses and running, laughing, playing with the fox just before he kills them. Running and running. I try to stop the fox, catch him, trap him, and then he turns on me and his jaws open.

I wake suddenly.

The thing beneath my ear is not a pillow and the stinking thing over my shoulders is not a blanket.

I turn and my head creaks.

This is not home.

This is a stable?

I try really hard to sit up but there's something

holding me down, which is when I realise that I'm tied to a bench and that my hands have fallen asleep by my sides and I can't feel my legs.

Perhaps it isn't a stable.

Above me, in the roof gable, a broken tile lets in a wash of morning light.

By tilting my head I can more or less see the whole room. It's probably an attic space; no proper windows, no real furniture. No stairs. Just very cold.

So how did this happen? I crawl through my memory. The assembly rooms, the questioning, the awful coach journey, the sharp woman, the dog.

The smell of vomit is still lurking in my nostrils. They gave me drink; it must've been in the tea and now I'm wrecked. My clothes are wrecked and I don't even know where I am. I don't even know what I said. But I've got that feeling of dread again. As if something's happened, or happening, and I'm not there to stop it.

Voices rumble beneath me, and something scrapes metal on wood.

"Let's take a look at him," says a voice I recognise.

The floor trembles against the bench and two shapes emerge from a trapdoor near my feet.

I close my eyes, pretending to still be asleep.

It's the Colonel and another man. He could be one of the men from the assembly rooms, but then again, he might not be.

They stand looking down on me. One on either side.

"Pitiful," says the Colonel in the end.

The other nods his head in agreement.

"What'll you do with him."

The Colonel rocks my head from side to side. I keep my eyes firmly shut. "Not sure," he says. "But I've an idea or two."

The other man giggles. "Like that auctioneer fellow?"

Blade clicks his tongue. "Mebbe, just like that auctioneer."

Their boots clunk on the boards and down the stairs and I listen to them disappearing, step after step, until I think they finally hit a stone floor. Mumbling floats up to me, a door slams and soon the house goes silent. So silent, I wonder if someone's sitting downstairs waiting. But then the light fades through the hole in the roof, and my bladder fills and I decide there's no one here, they've gone out.

They've left me.

Either because they want me to escape — or because they're sure I can't.

My head's clear now. But my arms have died on either side of me, so I begin to shift them, my elbow twitching, my wrist flicking, until the pins and needles race through my elbows and my hands begin to sting.

Keeping the movement going, I discover that my hands are tied together under the bench. I pull one; the other bumps into the wood under my thigh. If I stretch one arm under the bench, the other becomes looser, so I pull my shoulder blades together and bring my hands closer, until I feel the tension go out of the rope.

When we were little, Polly used to tie my hands together with the braid from the shop, and I would practise getting free in a matter of moments. It gave me hours of fun, and it drove her mad that she couldn't keep me out of the way.

I do the same now, twisting my thumb right inside my palm, until my hand becomes as thin as my wrist and slips out of the tie. The rope slides to the ground and my other arm bounces free.

Straight away I sit up, bringing my hands round, so that I can undo the remaining knot. The moment I'm free I reach for my feet, scrabbling with the rope, rubbing my ankles until I can move them again.

If I'm supposed to escape, then I'll do it as quickly as possible because I've just remembered something the Colonel said last night.

I know exactly how to get it.

He knows there's a way to crack me open, get me to give him the plans.

And I'm frightened that he's going to use it.

Shoeless, I pad over to the wall. Above me is the hole in the roof, black sky above, letting through a steady drizzle of snowflakes. Moving silently, I carry the bench over and stand it under the hole.

As I settle my foot on the bench, something about the house creaks and I pause, listening, but all I hear is the scuttling of rats. My fingers on the wall, I balance on the bench, sticking the top of my head through the hole. I can't see much, except blizzard, and the snow lands thickly on my eyelids, until I can't even see how much there is. Using my fingers to hold on to the shattered tiles on either side of the hole, I haul myself up until my head and shoulders are out and caught in the wind. I was cold already, but the wind is icy and I'm tempted to go back and find another way out.

But then, there could be someone downstairs.

One knee and then the other make it through the hole and I kneel sideways on the slates, looking over into a pit of swirling snow.

I sit for a minute trying to work out where I am. That might be a church tower over the right. And that dark shape to the left could be the top of the Octagon chapel. But it could be a tree.

Lying on my back, I reach my arms across the expanse of the roof and discover that there's a ridge above me, which I can just reach if I jam my feet against the hole and stretch.

It's cold – very cold – but my fingers grasp the ridge tiles and, thinking of my family, I pull myself backwards, up the roof, to the top and slip down the other side, against a chimney and out of the wind. Tugging my sleeves down, I pull up my collar and hunch my shoulders against the cold. I don't feel safe, I just feel safer. At least I can see anyone coming to get me through the hole in the roof, and I don't think there's any other way up here.

But I wonder if there's any way down.

Leaving the shelter of the chimney, I explore more of the roof. The snow drives at me, stinging my ears and slipping down the back of my neck, but I crawl over the slates until I find a small square flat area. Dropping down on to that, I find another roof. Larger and lower and suddenly I realise where I am.

New King Street. Near Mr Katz's house. Not far from home but I know from getting stuck up here a few years ago that it's not easy to get down off these houses, which is why Tod and I avoid them. Crouching, I map out the streets in my head.

There's a farm nearby with hayricks where I've

bought feed for Uncle's horses in the past, and I've got a feeling I'm very close by.

They keep horses there too, and a few cows, and I'm sure there's a dung heap. There has to be a dung heap.

Gusts of snow-filled wind sweep over the roof again so I turn my back against them and for a moment I'm lost; I can't work out which way I was going. I stumble about, blinded by the snow, my hands already so cold I can't feel them and my feet burning from the frozen tiles. My brain has frozen, thoughts barely moving.

A lump of ice from my stockings snaps off and falls, skittering across the slates and plummeting off the side of the roof.

I listen to hear it fall, but it doesn't make a sound.

Either it's so far down, the sound won't reach me, or there's something soft down there.

Lowering myself to my knees I peer through the snowstorm. Shapes and sounds.

Horses? Could that be horses stamping their feet in stables?

And could that mound covered in snow be the hayrick, or the dung heap?

I sniff the air – beyond the cold and fire soot, there's the smell of horses.

So I let myself go.

Chapter 20

Falling through the snowflakes, I wonder if I'm already dead.

That's all I've got time for.

Chapter 21

"Ugh."

Everything jolts, everything hurts. Opening my eyes I stare up at the dark snowfall.

I'm not dead then. Slowly I turn over and shake each limb. Nothing broken. The snow scrunches under my fingers, and below that, straw.

Frozen straw, but straw all the same.

I'm alive.

I'm still alive.

I let my feet over the side and slide to the ground. Never has the mud of a farmyard felt so good under my feet and I stand there, leaning against the hayrick breathing the thick cowy air and thanking Tod for the hours we've spent falling off roofs and surviving before picking my way over the frozen ruts and running out of the gateway.

Chapter 22

In the freezing dark I clamber up the drainpipe at the back of our house and in through Beatty's bedroom window. Inside it's even darker and she isn't here. I put my hands over her bed; it's still warm. From the floor I pick a paper bird. It's perfectly folded.

Moving along the unlit landing, I slip downstairs and into my room. My old clothes are lying there where I discarded them, dryer and cleaner than the ones I'm wearing, so I strip off the once beautiful jacket and my vomit-stained shirt and breeches, and seconds later I stand redressed, warm, in my old woollen coat.

A moment after and I'm on the landing, I check the parlour. The shutters are still open and slight snowlight makes the room glow, but it's empty. No sign of Grandma sleeping in the chair, no sign of anyone. Feeling the grate, I find it's cold. So no one's been in here at all today. I reach up behind the clock and find the sphere still there, warm and round and smooth.

But where is everyone?

Where's Ma?

Where's Polly?

Where's Beatty?

Downstairs, the shop's closed, and in the basement the range is almost cold. All the plates are tidied away as if no one's cooked. Ma's big coat's gone from the back of the door, and Polly's best boots from the fireside.

Even though it's dark and cold, I keep searching, as if I might find them hiding in the cupboard or under the table.

Only the ticking of the clock makes any sound. I've never known the house so quiet. I try to feel good. The plans are upstairs behind the clock. The secret's safe. But the quietness of our house worries me.

Where are they? In church? Surely they wouldn't

have taken Beatty — no one but me can carry her that far.

I know exactly how to get it.

Sick with fear I slip the bolts open on the kitchen door, and step back out into the night.

I miss the soft sounds of the hens as I pass the coop and I stand on a crate, listening. This time I'm sure there's no one here, no Colonel lurking. Clambering over the coal shed I step into the street and creep around to the Griffin.

The door's open a crack and Ma's laughter rings out from the warm yellow room. Quiet as a shadow, I sneak over the threshold. At the table where I first saw the Colonel, sit Ma, Grandma and Beatty. I rush forward, so glad to see them safe that I don't look properly.

I stop.

Caught half in, half out of the room.

The Colonel sits at the end of the table, cracking walnuts between his fingers.

He laughs and fills their mugs with something from a jug — his gold tooth shines in the candlelight.

"Athan!" shouts Beatty, curling her finger at me. "Where have you been? I thought the ghosties had taken you off."

They all turn to stare.

"Here, boy." Ma jams me on the bench next to her and whispers, "Colonel Blade's paying."

I plaster a grin across my face, determined not to show how worried I am to find this, all of them in his pocket. Ma, Grandma, even Beatty.

I settle myself between them. The Colonel looks at me unsmiling, his eyes hard and angry. Then he runs his tongue across his lips, like a man eyeing a tasty dish, and pulls a nasty smile. Ma prattles and giggles, and cuddles up to him. I move closer to Beatty.

"Where's Poll?" I whisper to her. "What's going on? What's he doing here?"

"It's all right. Poll's measuring in Brock Street." Beatty holds a mug of something steaming. Her eyes shine with excitement.

Grandma looks up from her mug. She frowns at me, sips a little and lays her head on the table.

Chatter flows over everyone. Ma's is louder than the rest and it all feels jolly – very jolly – but I rub my wrists where the ropes were and sneak a glance at the Colonel. He smiles and pours out cider and blows kisses at Ma. Beatty leans against me. "I thought you'd left me, Athan. I thought you'd deserted me."

"You know I wouldn't."

She doesn't answer. Instead she knots her fingers into mine, holding me tight.

The Colonel shifts himself into the light. He puts his hands together so that just the fingertips touch. They form a cage. Placing the hand cage over the candle he leers at me. The flame leaps up around his fingers but he doesn't move them. He keeps them there for minutes. Then slowly, like an executioner, he crushes the candle.

The flame dies; the hot wax flows out between his fingers.

Beatty sucks in her breath and stares. I do my best not to jump, but when I look up, his bright-blue eyes are gazing right at me. I glare back, feeling a flush of red creep up to my face. Beatty shakes beside me and I see that she's not touched her drink, but Ma's knocking it back, her face red and shining, her body squeezed into a silly new dress.

The Colonel picks wax from the hairs on the back of his hand. But he never moves his gaze from mine.

Deliberately, I look away. I try to seem unconcerned but I'm sure my face gives me away. Columbine Good sits in the fireplace. I notice her because for once she isn't drunk. She's a bundle of something wriggling at her feet. Kittens, for drowning, or puppies. She takes away the things that other people don't want and makes her living out of it. Anything. Kittens, puppies, ghosts, children. It's probably why she has to drink so much. She's watching our table with pinched eyes, following the chat and drinking nothing. Perhaps she's no money? For long minutes she gazes at the Colonel, her eyes narrowing and widening, her lips moving to a silent song.

Grandma's asleep. Her top lip trembles with each breath. In a moment, she'll start to snore.

Someone comes in behind us and the wind blows through the inn, whisking out the fug and filling the room with cold.

I turn. It's Mr Katz and his sister. They look out of place, but they stop at the bar and Mr Katz leans forward to talk to Peter the landlord.

They're buying wine.

"Now, Athan." Suddenly the Colonel's talking. "Athan knows summat about the sky. He knows how to get up there, don't you, lad?" I say nothing.

"Athan is just the man to take us on a tour of the heavens, so I suggest, madam," he holds out his hand to Ma, "that we take a little excursion to the yard of this fine hostelry to see the constellations."

Ma springs to her feet and takes his waxy hand, a beam of pleasure on her face. "Boy, do as the Colonel says."

"But what about Beatty?"

"Let her be, lad — child's not well enough to go

out stargazing." The Colonel leads Ma down to the steps at the back of the inn.

"Don't leave me here, Athan!" Beatty's arms reach out to me as she perches on the bench, her legs dangling into the dark.

I hesitate. "It's a public place. Grandma's here. And Mr Katz is over there."

Beatty's face wrinkles as she looks at Grandma, whose snores now echo from the walls. But she waves me away and I run to the back door.

We're out there for no more than a few minutes. Snow falls all around us, there's nothing to see, certainly no stars. The Colonel dances Ma twice around the yard, then stops and leads her towards me. I can't see his face in the chill dark. "So where's Venus then, lad?" he asks.

"Well, you can't see it," I reply. What's he up to?

"Up there I think you'll find her – god of love." He presses closer to Ma.

She giggles.

"And Mars, the god of war – just yonder." He points south. Does he really know what he's talking about?

"Oh, Colonel…" Ma says.

"Mordecai, call me Mordecai."

"Oh, Mordecai – you're so clever to know that. You

really are."

They stand so close together you'd struggle to put a blade of grass between them and I think of the sharp-faced woman and her wild looks and I see Ma, once fine but now a foolish shipwreck of a woman, and I hate him.

I clear my throat. They move apart. Ma puts her hand to her breast and laughs; the Colonel puts his arm through hers and leads the way back into the building.

I rush past them back to Beatty.

But she isn't there.

"Where's she gone?" I shake Grandma, but she spits out a glob of phlegm and looks muddled.

"Where's my sister?" I ask some men sitting in the window. They shrug and go back to drinking.

I look up towards the bar, where Mr Katz and his sister were a moment ago, but they've gone.

Ma stands there blinking in the middle of the room, looking around like she might find Beatty in the air. The Colonel runs to the door to look in the street.

"Where's she gone, Columbine?" Ma turns to the woman sitting in the fireplace.

But Columbine laughs and throws her apron over her head. "You've lost her, you've lost her, you've lost the little pearl. She wandered out with the fairies —

she's run away at last, the little changeling's going home."

Ma freezes and colour rushes into her face. She moves her head close to Columbine's. "Don't call my daughter a changeling! Shut your head, you daft creature, and start looking!"

"You know she's a changeling – left by the fairies to serve you right." Columbine rises to her feet. "It's for stealing men from other women's hearts. Twice." Columbine spits the last word.

"But I was going to send her to a hospital – they're going to make her better." Ma's face shakes with tears.

I look across to the Colonel. He gazes back. A smile plays over his lips and then he takes Ma by the shoulders.

"Don't worry, Moll. She'll be found. Athan'll find her. He knows how to get her back. Don't you, lad?"

And my blood freezes.

Chapter 23

Standing outside the inn, the snow settles on my face. Columbine staggers down the steps, the bag of mewling kittens slung over her shoulder. She stops, opens her mouth, closes it again and talks to the wall lamp.

"You, boy. You're a good lad."

"What?" I say. "Are you talking to me?"

"Maybe," she says. Pulling a half-toothed smile, then singing something, she disappears down towards the river, the darkness swallowing her whole.

I watch Columbine go, wondering if that meant anything.

I search the falling snow, as if Beatty could be out here somewhere. He took her from under my hand.

Unless.

The snow slows and I run on white carpets of it, newly fallen, covering the grimy streets until I reach Mr Katz's house.

He comes to the door himself.

"I am so sorry, Athan, but I have not seen your sister since we were in the Griffin Inn. She was sitting in the corner with your grandmother, and when we left she was still there." His face is very concerned and he looks as if he really does care where Beatty is.

"Thank you," I say. "But if you do hear anything?"

"We will keep a look out for her," he says.

Skidding through the whirling snow, I run to Tod's. His uncle stands over a coffin in the front yard, stuffing balls of cotton into a dead person's mouth. He nods to me as I come in.

It's colder inside than out.

"Tod back?" I ask.

"Receiving his just rewards," Mr Ballon sighs.

I look through the window. The workshop's only lit by a single lantern, but I can make out the scene straight away.

Tod's there, his arms braced over the back of a chair while his father cracks a broad leather belt. Tod's jacket hangs on a hook and he's only wearing a shirt, breeches and torn stockings.

"One!" bellows his father.

Thwack

"That's from your mother."

"Two!" The belt strikes again.

"And that's from me."

"Three!"

Thwack

"And that's from our Lord, for not honouring thy father and mother. Now, get out of here."

His father sinks on to the chair and reaches for a jug. Tod stays leaning, trembling, his hair touching his father's bald head. An odd sort of hiccupping sound fills the workshop and I realise it's Tod, crying.

I wait outside the door of the workshop for a minute, then knock and walk inside. Tod's father still sits in the chair and there's no sign of Tod himself. The man doesn't speak but waves me towards the wooden building at the back that passes as a kitchen.

Inside, Tod sits half naked and tear-stained before the empty fireplace, lighting a candle.

I don't know what say to him.

He looks up at me and grins. "I was fiddling about with the machine, stretching the wings out, working on some new spars. I forgot a funeral — they had to do it without me." His face is lined with tears.

"Tod, I'm dead sorry – I know, I mean I... Look – but he's stolen Beatty."

"What?" he says.

"Colonel Blade. He took them out to the Griffin. He took me prisoner but I escaped."

"Prisoner?"

"Yes, but that doesn't matter. Listen – it's him. He's taken her because he wants the plans."

"Well, give 'em to him."

My mouth drops open. "What? No!"

"Why not? What you got to lose?"

Why was Tod talking like this?

"Because – because I don't like bullies," I say. "And he's bullying me – and because Mr Chen hid it and died for it, because poor Mr Haddock, who knew nothing, died for it, and because if we win, that ten thousand guineas might change all our lives. It might cure Beatty, and get you out of here, and us out of there, and because you got beaten for it – and because, because – he wants it. And he's a cruel, brutal, awful monster of a man who'd use a crippled child..."

Tod leans forward and says a single word: "Beatty."

I stare at him for a moment.

"I've got to give him the plans, haven't I?"

Chapter 24

We agree that I'll offer Blade the plans in the morning. Which gives us until then to search the town, every inch of it. We meet the mad and the drunk, who laugh at our questions, but the street girls give us chocolate and promise to help.

In the early hours we run into Ma. She's in an awful mess, her hair all loose, her face ragged with crying.

"Polly's back at the house – in case." She leans on Tod.

"And the Colonel?" I ask.

"He's searching with the watchman. They're checking the rubbish pits." Ma falls into sobbing.

"My poor little girl, so tiny, all on her own. Whatever was I thinking – I can't possibly send her away, I can't live without her. The funny little thing."

We take Ma back to the house. I run upstairs into Beatty's empty room, where all that fills the space is a rag doll. I look at the place on her bed where she sits. It's the only space not dotted with paper birds. I pick up the doll and turn back downstairs.

Grandma sits in the drawing room with Polly. She's heating up blobs of sealing wax and dropping them into a cup of cold water. "Pigs – I see pigs," she says.

Ma just stares at her.

Grandma drops more wax in. "Oooh – devils – I see horns, and all sorts, terrible things."

I stand up and look over her shoulder. "I just see some red balls floating in a cup."

Ma presses her face into her hands and crumbles into tears. Polly comes over and gently strokes her cheek. Ma grabs Polly's hand and holds it close.

"Ma, I know who took her," I say.

Tod glares at me and shakes his head.

"Who?" She raises her eyes, and in the weak candlelight looks quite mad. "Was it Columbine?"

"No, not Columbine. She was still there after…" I reach towards Ma. "It's your sweetheart, Ma. Colonel Blade."

Her mouth falls open. For a moment she just stares.
The room goes pin silent.

Polly widens her eyes.

We wait.

When Ma speaks, her voice is barely above a whisper.

"Never, never talk to me like that again." She rises and walks to the fireplace. "Athan, I thought I'd brought you up properly — you mustn't do it — don't tell lies, and don't try and poison my mind."

"I'm not trying to poison your mind, I'm trying to tell you the truth." I reach out to her but she twists away. "He wants something, and Beatty's a tool — nothing more. He just wants to get hold of it."

"What?" she snaps. "What is it? What can it be that he'd take a child? How can you say that? How can you accuse such a gentle, kind man?"

Polly looks up at me and stares. Her eyes wide and clear and strong. She looks as if she's just understood something.

I reach up behind the clock. "This," I say, holding the ball out to them. "This is what he wants."

"What are you talking about?"

"It was Mr Chen's. Your Colonel, he wants it, and he murdered to get it. Now he's taken Beatty to force my hand."

They all stare.

Tod's jaw practically hits the floor.

"What is that thing, Athan?" asks Polly.

"It's a box, but I can't tell you what's inside. It would put you in danger – better you don't know."

"D'you mean—"

"Ha! More lies. Lies, lies, lies," interrupts Ma. "Nothing but lies. What did I do wrong to bring you up to be such a liar?"

I hold the ball up. "This is not a lie. This is a thing that could change the world. Your world, Ma. My world, Polly's world, Beatty's world."

"Won't change my world," mutters Grandma. "Not if it's anything to do with that—"

"Shut up!" Ma and Polly say together.

For a moment Ma looks at me. As if she might almost believe me and so I step closer. "Ma," I say quietly. "You're being led astray. We need to stand against him, keep him out."

There's a long pause. Ma turns to look at herself in the mirror. Bedraggled and undone, her hair hangs in wet coils, some stuck to her neck, the black around her eyes wandering madly down her face. The red of her lips has gone completely. "Lost two children, I have." She breathes in and her whole body shakes with sobs. "One to thieves, the other to lies."

"They're not lies, Ma. I'm not lying – that man's dangerous."

"Hush," she says. "Athan, Athan – you know he's the best thing to happen to me for years. How can you be so cruel?" Her eyes vanish behind the crying and I step forward to hold her, to hug her, but she pushes me away, me and Beatty's doll as if we're the worst things she's ever seen.

She turns and goes off up the stairs. Her soggy skirt thumping behind her.

From the top of the stairs, she shouts, "Go, boy. Go. Take that evil man's box out of this Christian house and don't come back until you've learned to tell the truth."

"C'mon," says Tod from behind me. "You can't do nothing about it."

"What d'you do that for?" asks Tod as we leave the house.

"I don't know," I say, shoving the ball deeper in my pocket. "I hoped she might believe me."

"Stop!" shouts a voice from behind us, and Polly comes clattering down the street, her skirts held up around her waist. "Athan," she pants. "What's going on?! What is that thing – I want to know and I want to know now!"

Todd goes to check the timber yards on his way home. Me and Polly stand shivering in an alley, a dusting of grey daylight snow falling all around us as the church bells strike eight.

"Well?" she says. "Tell me."

"From the beginning?" I say.

She nods.

I check the alley, and down the street, and listen hard for footsteps.

"C'mon, Athan, tell me before we both freeze to death."

I take a deep breath, and start talking. "Mr Chen and me, we built a flying machine."

"Oh, Athan," she gasps, slapping her hand over her mouth. "How wonderful!"

"And there's a prize, as you know."

"Ten thousand guineas, in the paper."

"Yes, but the Colonel must have got wind of it — he's after it. So he's taken Beatty to make me give him the flying machine."

Polly shakes her head. "So he's not Ma's shining prince then," she says after a million snowflakes have landed on us.

"No," I say. "He almost certainly murdered Mr Chen and Mr Haddock, and tried to murder Uncle."

Polly shivers. "So he did all that to get his hands

on this machine. Which you're going to give him," she says.

"I'm going to give him the plans for it," I say, rolling the ball around my pocket.

With her toe, she traces a circle in the snow.

"But I'm not going to give him the actual machine."

"Why ever not?"

"He doesn't know about it. We could build it, get it up in the air, get the prize while he's still puzzling out the drawings. They're all in Chinese anyway. It'll take him ages."

A carriage rattles past over the cobbles, the horses skidding on the ice and the coachman shouting.

"So you're thinking that you hand over the plans to this murderer, and he gives back Beatty."

"Yes." I nod.

Polly gazes off down the street, the snowflakes eddying and landing on her thick hair until she looks like some kind of snow princess.

"He might not," she says.

"He'll have to, or I won't give them to him."

Polly twists her mouth. She's finding the holes in my plan but I can't afford to let her.

"It'll work," I say.

"How are you going to do it then?"

"I need to get him to give me proof that Beatty's

still alive first. And then arrange for the handover to be in a public place – like the assembly rooms, or by the abbey." I'm making it up as I go along.

She knows I am and sucks snowflakes off a strand of hair.

"Is there anyone you could use as a go-between – a reliable person? So there's less chance of the Colonel double-crossing you?"

Straining to think of someone, I remember Mr Katz. I don't know him well but he's sound. "There is," I say. "I could ask that Beatty be left there, and give the plans over to him to pass on."

"Hmmm," she says.

"What?" I say.

"You're taking a big chance, Athan," she says eventually. "If you're right, and the Colonel killed Mr Chen, how do you know he didn't find out about the machine? How can you be so sure? He might be after much more."

I watch her go back inside the house, and shortly afterwards the Colonel crosses from one house to the other, smiling, walking easily with long loping strides. I think he knows I'm watching him. And it doesn't bother him one bit.

Although I'm tired, I know that whatever happens

176

we have to get on with the machine and, struggling up into Tod's loft, I catch him fast asleep at his desk.

"We've got to get it finished," I say, lugging the soggy structure through the window and into his workshop.

"Oh, Athan." he says, rubbing his eyes. "No trace of Beatty, by the way – I asked in the timber yards."

"You won't find her – he's hidden her well. Anyway, we need someone who can sew," I say. "And not Polly – he's going to have his eyes on her."

"What are you on about?" Tod staggers to his feet and sits down again. "Thought if we couldn't find her you were going to deliver the plans?"

"I will, I will, but Polly's going to talk to the Colonel, try to get proof that Beatty's still alive first. That buys us a few hours, but once they have the plans they'll build it in days – if we're going to win the prize we need to beat them to a finished machine."

"If you say so," says Tod.

"The engine's more or less sorted. But Mr Chen and me, we never attached the silk to the frame properly. We kept trying with glue, but it needs sewing together. Neat little stitches, not the kind of thing I'd do. Small stitches are stronger."

"I'm no good for that," says Tod, attempting to stretch the wet fabric over the wooden frame. "Nor's anybody here."

"Do you think Mary would do it?" I ask.

Tod looks at his boots. "You could ask her."

I remember what Polly said about go-betweens. "Right," I say. "I will. And while I'm gone, see if you can work out a way of attaching the engine to the frame."

"Yes, sir," says Tod, taking a bite out of an apple and sitting back down on the floor.

The shutters are open on the Katz house and I slip around the back, up over the garden wall and down again, so that I can catch Mary in the kitchen.

"Oh, Athan!" she says, sitting down suddenly in a chair. "You gave me a turn."

"I want to ask you a favour."

There's a warm pie, just out of the oven, and the smell is almost unbearable. I can't keep my eyes from it. I must make it too obvious because Mary covers it with a cloth and sticks it out of sight, but I can still smell it.

"You know about Beatty," I say.

"Is she still missing?" she asks.

"Yes, and we know who took her and why."

"Tell the constable," she says.

"No, I can't prove it, but we can get her back – I'm sure of it. It's just that we need someone who can sew really well."

"How on earth is sewing going to help get your baby sister back?"

"It's not."

"I don't understand you, Athan. What about Polly? She's the best seamstress in town."

I shake my head. "No – she can't. It's too dangerous. But I wondered if you could?"

She tilts her head to look at me. "Too dangerous for your own sister, but you'd ask me?"

"I don't think you'd be in danger – it's just Polly."

Mary puts her hands on her hips and frowns. "Athan Wilde, you make no sense and you've told so many stories in your time I don't know whether to believe you or not."

"I know it doesn't make sense, but I really need your help. And – I might need Mr Katz's help. If you think he'd be open to a proposition?"

Mr Katz is in his drawing room. Drawing.

He has a huge piece of paper and he's scribbling on it and drawing lines from one point to another and measuring stuff. He rolls it up as we step through the door, pushing up his sleeves, and looking, for the first time since I met him, irritated.

Mary bobs in the doorway and stands aside and

I hover, uncertain. "Mr Katz, sir," I begin.

"Mr Wilde, how can I help you?"

"My sister Beatty, the one who disappeared from the inn – do you remember?"

"Yes," he says. "I remember you coming here to look for her."

"Well she's been kidnapped."

"No!"

"I know what the kidnapper wants and I need to swap Beatty for it. But I want her to be safe, so—"

"What?" says Mr Katz, staring at me, his face almost radiant.

"So I wondered if I could do it here – give you the thing that the kidnapper wants, and get him to leave Beatty here."

Mr Katz bows deeply. "I would be honoured," he says, "to be your broker."

It must be Mr Katz agreeing that makes Mary agree, and she follows me back to Tod's loft, her skirts bundled up so that they don't trail in the slushy snow. She talks all the way, but I don't really listen. I'm thinking how straightforward it all seems.

Mr Katz agreed so easily; he didn't even ask when it might happen.

Wonderful.

If the swap goes ahead, and Mary sews the fabric on the bird, then we'll have Beatty back in a trice and we'll just be trying to launch it. I wonder how you win the prize.

"So what is it I'm sewing?" says Mary, bumping her elbow into mine.

"I'll show you when we get there," I say.

"Tod's loft?" she asks. "I've been up here before."

"Have you?"

"I'm friends with Tod, you know," she says, fixing me with her eel-brown eyes.

Friends? "So did you know about the kite?" I ask, embarrassed and trying not to show it.

She tilts her head from side to side. "Sort of. Have you got the plans with you?"

"Shh," I say. We stop at the coffin yard.

"I can't climb up in these skirts," she says. "Have to go the proper way."

The door stands a crack open so we peer around it. It's dark inside, but a single candle illuminates what's going on. Tod's uncle leaning over a tiny coffin, pouring something down a funnel.

"Oh Lor'," says Mary. "He's pickling the poor mite – Tod says he likes to experiment with the little ones." She shudders. "He wants to make the bodies last longer so they can stay in an open box."

"Hello!" I say, pushing the door open wide and looking away from the coffin. "We've come to see Tod, if we may."

Mr Ballon's mournful face looks up at us. His eyes so dark I can't see them, sunken deep in the white skin.

I don't know how Tod lives here, his uncle like a living corpse, his father a thug. And so cold, this place is so cold.

Mary bobs a greeting and we push on through to the tiny kitchen and up the ladder to Tod's loft.

Tod's folded the kite over to one side and has laid all the pieces of the engine across the floor.

"Ah – Athan, I need to ask you how this bit moves." He holds up the wooden fan. "Does it fit in here?"

For an hour or more, we work like demons. I take the plans from the ball and stretch them across the table. Mary and Tod pore over them, and I explain and point and tap the engine together.

"What's this?" asks Mary, pointing to a square of red script in the top corner.

"Dunno, can't read Chinese," I say.

"It's not in Chinese, it's in English," says Mary.

"Ah, of course," I say. I exchange looks with Tod. Neither of us can read.

"Oh," says Mary. "It's to you, Athan."

"What does it say?" asks Tod.

Mary leans over the plans, her mouth moving as she sounds out the letters. *"Dear Athan,"* she begins slowly. *"If you are reading these plans, you have found what I knew you would find because you are persistent and clever. I am hiding them because I think we have been found out. I believe that there are other people after our machine, and that they may use any means to get it. I want you to guard it with your life, but no more. Don't put your family at risk, your enchanting sisters or your splendid mother. Better to give in gracefully than to let them suffer.*

"But I like to think that you and our bird will some time fly free, and take humanity a step further.

"Your friend, Isaac Chen."

"Isaac?" says Tod. "I never had him down as an Isaac."

I can't speak. I try to sniff as quietly as I can, but obviously do a poor job of it because Mary takes a perfectly laundered handkerchief out of her sleeve and passes it to me.

"My pa was a maker," she says cheerfully. "He taught me lots of things when I was little, but this is remarkable, I'd love to show Mr K – he'd be dead impressed."

"Don't think you better had," I say. "Better not to know anything about it in my experience."

"No," she laughs. "It's not been a lucky machine, has it?"

We all fall silent and stitch and screw and tap.

"I'd better go and see Polly," I say in the end. "See what she's found out."

I clamber over the yard wall, brushing a parapet of snow on to the abandoned hen boxes. From the kitchen door, I can see Polly standing over the range, two little spots of pink on her cheeks.

Tapping gently on the grimy glass, I wait for her to let me in.

"Oh, Athan – it's awful," she says in a whisper. "Grandma's already sleeping in your bed. She's been chanting spells and laying garlic in the doorways."

"So soon?" I shudder.

"And I never realised how much Ma loves you both. She's wept all night, she won't eat. She's grieving. Anyone would think you were both already dead."

She's struggling not to cry. "I'm sorry, Poll," I say, reaching my arms around and holding her scrawny shoulders. "It won't be for much longer – I'm going to get her back, today. I promise."

She nods and sniffs and wipes her hands on her apron. "And that stupid stove – I can't get it to light." She almost laughs, swiping a tear with the back of her hand, leaving a coal smut across her cheek.

"It's a beast," I say.

"Could you?" she asks.

"Course," I say, stepping over and opening the clinker drawer. A tiny flame licks over the paper. "Did you talk to the Colonel?"

"I did. I said, imagine – if someone was holding Beatty, to get something from us, how would we know if she was still alive?" The fire grabs hold of a splinter of wood and sputters into life.

"And?"

"He dropped that round, just now." She points to the table. "Brought it down here to the kitchen and handed it to me."

"He's not still here?"

She shakes her head. "It's today's," she says.

A rolled-up newspaper.

I flick through it until the centre pages fall open. There, right in the middle, one of Beatty's birds and a hand print. A small, reddy-brown hand print.

I cough and drop the paper.

"What is it?" Polly runs to me. She picks up the bird from the floor. "One of Beatty's birds? Oh my Gods – is that what I think it is?"

I shake my head. I don't trust myself to speak.

"Oh!" Her voice drops away.

"I was hoping you were wrong." She speaks so low

I barely hear her. "But you were right."

I nod.

She turns away. "The devil!" She spits the words.

I persuade Polly to write a note for me.

6pm Mr Katz's house. New King Street.

That should give us long enough to get every scrap from the plans.

After posting the letter through his door, I run down through the slithery streets to the loft and shin up the back. I can't bear to walk through the coffin yard more often than I have to.

Inside, Mary's fingers are flying over the cloth and Tod's done a sound job of fixing the engine underneath.

"What we missing then?" he says.

And I draw up a list.

When the church strikes five, Mary sits back, her fingers red with stitching.

"I've got to go and prepare the dinner," she says.

Folding the plans, I jam them into the ball and click it shut.

"Would you carry it? And I'll come just behind," I say. "In case he decides to jump me for it."

Mary looks alarmed.

"You'll be all right," says Tod. "He's no idea who you are."

Mary blenches and reaches out and tucks the ball into her cloak. "And you'll be right behind me?" she says.

"Yes," I say. "And we can run if you like. It's not very far."

"I'd go in through the front door," she says.

"So will I then."

The streets are frozen and dark as we step out of the coffin yard. Mary walks ahead of me, the ball invisible under her cloak, and I walk about twenty yards behind.

It's time for the evening service so there are people around, mostly scuttling over packs of ice and wagon tracks as quickly as they can, so I don't think I look as if I'm following her.

As we approach the house I hold back and see her safely in before I run the last few feet and crash through the door.

"Ah – young Mr Wilde, how are the plans progressing?" For a moment I think Mr Katz is talking about the kite and then I realise he isn't.

"Beatty will be brought here at six. Mary?"

She pulls the ball from her pocket and hands it to

him.

"What is this?" he says.

"It was Mr Chen's," I say. "You don't need to know more than that."

He rolls the ball from one hand to the other, examining the stars. "Beautiful craftsmanship," he says. "I should love to know what it is for."

I clear my throat. "I'm sorry, I can't tell you that. But the man you're waiting for is a Colonel Blade."

"Colonel Blade," Mr Katz repeats.

"Yes, and he should bring Beatty here in about half an hour."

"Good," says Mr Katz, smiling. "Now, off you go. Mary, you stay in the kitchen."

"I was going to watch from the other side of the road – from the rooftops."

Mr Katz pinches his lips. "I think it would be foolish. I think you should be well away from here. In case he sees you."

"I'll make sure he doesn't."

Mr Katz tilts his head. "Do you think he works alone?"

I think of the sharp-faced woman, and the men at the assembly rooms. "No – I think there are other people."

"In that case he'll have someone watching the house.

You will be spotted."

He stands in the hall, the ball in his hand and his sleeves rolled up, and I suddenly worry that another person's been caught up in all this who doesn't deserve it.

"Thank you, Mr Katz."

He bows.

I bow.

"And be careful, Mr Katz, very careful."

"And you, young Mr Wilde. You too."

I walk through the streets. I'm sure I'm watched. Mr Katz is right, I need to be seen to leave. And then, when I get down to the Griffin Inn I throw myself through the front door, fight my way through the drunks, out the back and shimmy up a drainpipe.

I pause on the roof, looking down into the street.

There's no one I could identify as the men from the assembly rooms, but then, there are plenty of people down there muffled from the cold who I can't recognise. Crouching in the snow shadow of a chimney I try to see what's going on in New King Street, but I can't see far enough.

Carriages come and go.

Sedan chairs come and go.

From the pub I pass the stained-glass windows of a

chapel and pick my way over a rotten warehouse until I reach a row of houses that give me a good view.

Still nothing to see though.

Bong

Bong

The abbey clock strikes half past.

I wonder if that's long enough.

Tucking my hands under my armpits for warmth I wait, and watch and wait until the abbey's bells strike seven.

Then I clamber down and head up the town towards New King Street.

"He didn't leave Beatty?" I say, staggering back against the wall.

Mr Katz holds his hands out. "He showed her to me, from a carriage, so I know she is well. She waved at me. He started to help her down, so I handed him the ball, and then he pushed her back inside and the coach took off again. I am devastated."

Above me a lamp flickers and I stare at it to stop myself bawling.

"Thank you for trying," I say. And I head out into the darkness.

"Oh, Athan," says Tod.

"I know," I say, tapping the fan into the engine and tightening the screw.

We work on in silence.

The kite looks almost ready. No way to launch it, without the wind in the right direction, but it's almost ready and it fills Tod's loft like a giant pink moth.

"Looking good, isn't it," says Tod. "Like a proper air carriage. Do you think he knows we've built it?"

"I don't know. I can't guess." I snap. "But whatever he thinks, I'm going to look for some spirits of vitriol for the spark," I say, grabbing my jacket and heading out into the freezing night.

Trying to think of a way to find Beatty, I stumble out to Uncle's farm. Frozen ruts, almost knee-deep, catch me as I walk and it's hard going.

Skidding on the pond I find myself quite suddenly by the deserted barns and, feeling my way in the dark, find Uncle's wagon, still full of stuff from the day we emptied Mr Chen's house. I can't see a thing, but with my hands I trace the shapes. Without light, I can't tell which containers hold the vitriol, so I fumble around until I find a wheelbarrow and carefully load it up with all of them.

I push a flea-bitten blanket into the gaps and I wheel the barrow out, away from the farm but not straight towards the city, because I know I won't be able to get it over the ruts. Instead I head south, where there's a stone track and I can use it to get up towards Tod's loft.

It takes all night. But my anger keeps me awake and strong so I don't even feel tired, though I still don't know what to do about Beatty. With dawn, a strong cold wind picks up and it scours the river, rippling the oil patches on the surface that shine like metal under the grey light.

I look up at the city. I've hardly ever seen it from this side.

The backs of the buildings are rough with mortar and rubble stone; boat houses and warehouses falling into the water, propped up by rubbish and luck. Buildings stretch up into clouds, their tops lost in the mist, their feet standing in river fog.

Something blows on the damp wind and lands on the water. A leaf? Then another, and a third.

Looking at the river I see the surface is littered with a line of tiny spiky things. They're floating on down to Bristol, masses of them.

They look like folded shapes.

Hundreds of them, litter the surface.

Floating damp swans in the river – coming from the town.

Paper birds?

They ride the air like dandelion seeds and I follow them back to their beginning. There, stuck to the gutters of an old boat house, a cluster. Peppered around the high window, tiny shapes in all colours.

Beatty's paper birds.

Are they real?

I shiver in a mixture of fear and hope, put down the barrow and close my eyes. Then I look again.

They're still there, masses of them, and now I see they're plastered to the river bank below and to the mud.

She's been flying them out of the window. She's sent me the same message a thousand times and finally I've seen it.

I stare and as I stare another bird whisks out of the window of the building and floats slowly down to land on the water.

Abandoning the barrow I run over to cross the bridge away from the city. From here I can see better. It's an isolated building, backing on to the river. I don't think I even knew it was there. For a moment I watch. Two more birds fly out of the dark square. One plummets and dies in the mud below, the other floats, flying free on the air before escaping on the river.

Traders are pouring into the city so I dodge between

them, skipping over the ruts and mud, my hopes bouncing with me, making me skip higher and higher until I practically fly up to the loft.

"I've found Beatty," I announce to Tod. "I know where she is!"

Tod's fitting the electric box into a little basket under the kite and he stops to look at me, a piece of wire dangling from his mouth.

"What? You're kidding! Where?"

"By the river. She's been sending birds – those paper birds of Mr Chen's."

"C'mon then," says Tod, dropping the wires and grabbing his coat. "No time to waste."

Chapter 25

We need Mary again to make the plan work.

"So you'd get me to risk my life so that we can save her — is that right?"

"Yes," I say. "Just about. Tod's risking his too."

Tod smiles. "Willingly."

She reaches into a bucket where a fish is flopping. "He's a fool, isn't he. Look at him — his eyes are too close together and he can't tie his laces properly."

Tod blushes and looks down at his feet. He loves her, I know it, and I think she loves him back but she's got a funny way of showing it.

"But, Mary, we can't do this without you, honest.

You're the only one Colonel Blade doesn't know. Please. There may only be hours left before he…"

"If you want to know the truth, I'm scared." She whacks the fish's head on the draining board. Her face is as sour as it used to be at the Benefis school.

I smile in the warmest way I can manage, but I expect it looks false. "Please?"

She sighs and sprinkles the fish with flour. It flaps away until Tod grabs it and whacks its head on the side of the sink. "Very well, for your sister — but so long as you know."

I know she's scared. We all are.

The town's teeming. Mary walks ahead. Tod and I creep between doorways like street thieves.

She gets down to the abbey and we cross behind her on Orange Grove, skirting the Frappels coffee house before stopping. There, in the street, stands Colonel Blade.

His back is to us and he's talking to someone inside the coffee house, but I can't see who. There's a slatted screen between them.

Squeezing myself under a cartload of cabbage I listen. I can't hear very much over the market people calling to one another but I can catch the odd word.

Tod opens his mouth. I press my finger against my

lips and he squeezes in next to me. Mary slides into the shadow of the abbey. I hope she'll wait.

"How d'you mean?" Blade says.

He listens intently and a small flicker of a smile crosses his lips, but he wipes it away with the back of his hand and taps his heel on the ground.

"So what d'you want done? The boy's given us the plans. What more can I do?"

I listen really hard for the other voice but I can't catch it at all.

"So you just want me to stop him?"

He listens.

"And if he won't – you want him dead?"

He listens, smiles, and a little muscle in his cheek clicks on and off, on and off.

Then he breathes in before letting out a slow long sigh, as if he's making a great concession. "I'll get your machines, or stop the little devil making his. But this time I'll do it my own way and damn the consequences – for you and for me." He turns and set off at a trot.

Oh God. Where's he going? I glance back at the coffee shop; there's not time to see who he's been talking to. I follow the Colonel, Tod by my side. Turns out, Mary hasn't waited.

It soon becomes clear he's on his way down to the

house by the river.

"Lumme," Tod says, touching my elbow. "He wasn't part of the plan."

I shake my head. We'd had it all worked out: Mary was going to knock on the door and keep whoever was in the house busy with her basket of charity food, while Tod and I nipped up and grabbed Beatty through the window, and got away before she was missed.

We hadn't bargained on the Colonel being there.

We catch sight of Mary where the town gives way to rubbish heaps that lead down to the river. I want to warn her, tell her that she doesn't have to do it, but she marches on, close behind the Colonel.

As we approach the river, the mist thickens, so that our feet disappear beneath the whiteness and our shins seem to sprout from nowhere. The Colonel strides ahead while Mary moves carefully behind him, her umbrella pulled close down to her face. Smoke from the rendering sheds between the warehouses coils up to mix with the mist, and the smell of damp charcoal and old meat fat is so strong I have to pull my scarf over my nose.

Tod slips down behind a wall a few yards from the river. I crouch next to him. The warehouses hang above us and there isn't much to them. They're really boat sheds, more river and rot than roof and walls.

You can see right through some of them.

The Colonel makes for the biggest building and crashes in through the door. Everything shakes.

We hear him climb the stairs.

"You don't have to do this," I hiss at Mary, who is standing in the open, apparently frozen to the spot.

She doesn't respond. Under the flaps of her bonnet her pretty face is white, her eyes wide. She's terrified but she steps forward to the door.

"C'mon." Tod pulls at my arm. I duck around to the north side of the warehouse; he vanishes to the south. Mary has to wait five minutes then knock.

"That's it! I've had enough," I hear the Colonel shout. "I'll wring his bloody sister's neck, the little runt. Double cross me, would 'e? They're no more use as the plans for a flying machine than I'm the King of England." He stamps on the wooden boards. "And when I've throttled 'er – I'll get me the next size up! Fetch the little pixie for me now, woman!"

I stop.

"Don't speak to me like that! You – you!"

It's the sharp-faced woman and she's angry. There's the sound of a struggle and I run, scrambling along the outside of the building, up and up. Beatty must be at the top where the paper birds are.

"Don't you get uppity with me, you stupid cow!"

More struggling and someone thumps into the side of the building, and a slap.

"Oh!" the woman yells. "You brute!"

Then the sound of Mary knocking on the door rings through the whole building. The shouting stops.

A chain rattles and I haul myself up on to a gantry that runs across the riverside of the building. Tod's foot appears at the other end. We're climbing neck and neck, hand over hand. I reach up for a gutter, which comes away in my hand, so I throw it clear into the river. It splashes.

Soon I hear feet pounding on the stairs. Mary can't have stopped them for long then.

I speed up. Above me is the window, plastered in the paper birds, but everything's spongy under my fingers and it stinks of fish and tar and mushrooms. The wood is so rotten, I've nothing to hang on to.

"Beatty?" I call up, as loud as I dare.

"Athan? Are you there?"

I could cry. It's her all right. "I'm here, me and Tod, we're coming, just stay tight." But I can't see how. How can we possibly get there? It's like climbing through cake; it falls away in my hands. I poke a plank – my nail goes right through it. I poke another; it's the same.

From the other side of the hole, Beatty giggles. Her little finger pushes through from inside and the wood crumbles down past my feet. Tod hauls up next to me and together we pull a plank away. And another. It comes apart like a boiled egg shell, with each piece showing just a little more of Beatty sitting on the floor inside.

"Yes, yes!" She claps, her eyes bright, her face thinner than ever. "I'm a bird and you can take my nest from me, yes, yes!"

The door to her room rattles. A key screeches in the lock.

We've a hole in the side of the room. We can see Beatty but there's nothing to hold on to. Leaning on the strongest piece of wood that I can find, I slip my arm in and pull Beatty's legs out through the gap.

The door grates across the floor.

Tod takes one of Beatty's arms, I take the other and we balance on the tops of the windows from the floor below, teetering over the brown rushing water, held in place by our fingertips embedded in the spongy wall.

"What the—" It's the Colonel, he's in the room behind us.

Tod shoots me a glance then looks down at the water. I nod.

"Fly, Athan, fly!" shouts Beatty, and we throw ourselves off.

Chapter 26

We take what seems like minutes to hit the water, and when we do it sucks all the air from my chest and leaves me struggling to keep afloat. And then I don't keep afloat any more, I go under. Beatty's dress blows out around me. Through it I grip her skinny arm and I don't let go even though we seem to be going down and down and I haven't got a scrap of air left. We hit the bottom of the river and we're tossed round and round, bounced and dragged across the mud, and still I hold on to Beatty. And then I hit a rock and must let go of her because I can't feel the cloth any more. I thump to the bottom and push up, kicking off my boots, swimming hard and breathless, sure that what I can see of the sky through the muddy water is my last sight ever on the Earth, until suddenly I'm at the surface, gasping and sucking the air in and swimming against the stream.

Crack

Crack

Spouts of water leap into the air in front of me. I struggle around and gaze back towards the warehouse.

The Colonel's balanced on a beam, a gun up against his shoulder, firing at us.

"Athan!" shouts Tod, clinging to a boulder of mud on the side. "Where the heck's Beatty?"

"Has she not come up?" I shout.

"No."

I plunge back down under the thick grainy water. Things thump into my sides and drape themselves around my face. I imagine the foul stuff that the nightmen dump in the river and the dead creatures washed in by the snow melt, the rats and the offal, and clamp my mouth shut as I dive down wafting my arms from side to side, searching for any trace of Beatty. My knuckles strike the bottom of the river again; stones and soft horrible mud slide over my hands, and my fingers grab things that give way in my grasp. I push up from the bottom, reaching for the air, and on my way something made of cloth brushes my face. I grab it and push hard with my feet, kicking and kicking, dragging and pushing it up above my head. It's so heavy, this bag of cloth, it surely can't be Beatty, but I yank at it, pushing and pulling, my lungs bursting and shrinking until someone else is tugging and the material floats all around us and we're back up in the flow and the drizzle's falling on my face.

Crack

"Pwaah!" Tod bounces out of the water next to me, Beatty's seaweed hair stuck to his face, her face white next to his, but her eyes open.

Crack

The Colonel fires again; this time the bullet bounces right in front of my nose.

Crack!

I strike out, grasping a handful of her dress, and Beatty's tiny arms flap, but I can't tell if it's her or the river moving them. The current's fast and Tod loses his grip, swept on beyond us. Beatty's dress threatens to pull us out into the stream but I fight for the bank even though I can no longer feel my arms or legs, and only the sight of my own hand gripping hers tells me that I've still got her.

We've drifted so far downstream that I can make out the main horse bridge into the town right in front of us. The winter storms have filled the arches on the right with broken trees and fallen branches, forming a dank wooden island. If we can stay afloat and head to the right, we'll arrive with the other rubbish and not get sucked underneath. I try to pull my legs up to the surface, stretching as flat as I can, pushing Beatty sideways so that we take up the longest area and have the best chance of hitting the bridge itself. We float on the brown river, and at the last second a current bounces us towards the debris, until with an iron blow my shoulder hits a tree trunk and we stop. Tod drifts to the next island of twigs, his clothes all brown with river mud, his hair the same.

I stay there, clinging to Beatty, rubbing at her face and sucking in great wonderful mouthfuls of air. Sooty, coally air, but air all the same. Beatty's face is cold, her eyes are closed, her arms icy. I lift her arm, it falls back, limp. Oh no, not after all this. I pinch her cheek. Her eyes open and slide towards me.

"Athan," she says. "I knew you'd come."

It takes me an age to climb from the river. No one helps; they hurry on by as if mud-brown people clamber from the water every day. I look back towards Tod and notice that he hasn't moved since he hit the bridge pillar.

I drag Beatty on to the cobbles; she's grey from head to toe and shivering. She looks like a ghost.

"Where's Tod?" she says, jamming her hands under her armpits for warmth.

"I'll get him," I say.

Staggering to the side, I lean over the parapet of the bridge. Tod's still there, wedged in the branches.

"Tod!" I shout. "Get up, you silly beggar! You'll freeze to death."

His head lifts and falls again. He doesn't turn to face me.

"Tod!" I shout.

Beside me a drover stops and peers over. "He's not moving," he says. "Looks dead to me."

"No," I say. "Can't be. Give me a hand."

Together we reach down and pull Tod from the water; he doesn't resist. He doesn't help.

"Tod," I say. "Come on, wake up."

He's really heavy and the drover's sweating by the time we get Tod up and we all collapse back on to the cobbles, water streaming from our clothes.

And then I see it. On Tod's chest, a red flower, growing. I tear the sleeve from my shirt and hold it over the blood, pressing down, but I don't know if it works with a bullet hole. I've never seen a bullet hole before.

"Tod," I say. "Open your eyes!"

"He's been shot," says the drover. "How's that then?"

"Quick, call someone – get a surgeon! Tod!"

"Let me see," says Beatty, crawling across.

"Oh!" she says, pulling the hair from Tod's face. "I'm here too, Tod," she says.

"Beatty," he says, his tongue slow, a slight smile on his face. "Glad we could—"

"Tod!" she shouts. "Tod – wake up!" And then she goes quiet.

I look down at the shirt in my hand. The blood's soaked it, but there doesn't seem to be any more.

"Tod?" I say quietly, just as the drover returns with a woman I recognise as a midwife. She leans over and puts her finger to Tod's throat, her face serious.

Beatty looks up at her; they nod at each other.

"He's dead, Athan," says Beatty. "Tod's dead."

Chapter 27

I wait to see the river men hoist Tod on to a cart, watching all the time through tears that wash the mud from my face on to Beatty's. We stand shivering and grey in the rain, clutching each other, while a crowd forms around us.

"He's the lad from the coffin yard," says a big man, stopping to see Tod laid straight.

"Shame," says a woman. "Young man like that."

"Shot?" says a man.

"In this town?" says another.

They cover him with a horse blanket. His skin's grey; he looks as if he's been dead for hours but I

208

know it's a matter of minutes. The red smudge on his chest is the only damage.

"He must have got into trouble." A woman peers at the wound.

"He didn't," says Beatty. "He was saving me — he died saving me." But she doesn't say any more. Unusually for Beatty, she's lost for words.

I feel as if I've been punched. As if my whole world is destroyed.

Chapter 28

We see Tod back into the coffin yard, his body laid gently in the embalming room, his father called and the awful grief that it unleashes. Beatty clings to me and I to her, and for an hour or two I can't remember what I'm doing or what I want to do.

Tod's uncle ushers us out. "I need to wash him," he says, his face older and sadder than I've ever seen.

"Home?" says Beatty.

Our house is draped in black. The shop window is closed off with black bombazine curtains hanging over the door. Beatty shivers on my shoulders as we walk up the hill.

"Why's home all black, Athan? Do they know about Tod?"

"They think you're dead," I answer.

"Me?" Beatty pushes her hands down over my eyes. "But I'm not!"

"I know," I say, taking her hands off my eyes again. "But Ma thinks you are."

"Oh!" Again, Beatty's stuck for words.

We stop outside for a moment. The house opposite's all shut up, no smoke from the chimneys, the shutters closed. So where's the Colonel now? I hesitate outside the door but Beatty's shivering so much that I'm going to have to take her in, no matter who's there.

I wish Tod was with us.

"Open the door," I whisper to Beatty.

She leans down and turns the handle and the door swings open. The shop's empty.

We stay on the mat, water still dripping from our clothing, and listen. There are rumbling voices overhead and the floor's creaking, but there's no noise coming up from the kitchen.

"Where are they gone to?" Beatty asks, pulling herself closer to my neck.

"Shh," I say, edging across the floor towards the basement stairs. We take ages to go down, not a squeak or a creak giving us away. When we finally reach the kitchen we stop in the doorway blinking and staring at Polly leaning over the stove, her face red in the firelight.

"Poll," I whisper.

She turns and drops the kettle. "Oh God! Oh Lord – Beatty!" She runs forwards and holds us both, making herself all muddy at the same time. "Oh Lord – oh my goodness!" she gasps. She sits back on a chair and fans her face with her hand, her eyes not leaving Beatty's for a moment.

"Who's up there?" I point.

"Ma, Grandma. They're getting in touch with the dead. Oh, I can't believe it!" She springs up and hugs Beatty even closer, and Beatty clings to Polly's bodice, her grubby hands twisted into the black cloth. "And Mrs Love from over the road is there, they're drinking tea with crab paste toast and seed cake. I was just making another pot." Her face twists into something between tears and laughter. "And you're all wet! Wherever have you been?"

"We jumped into the river and Athan got us out. Tod's dead."

"What?" says Polly.

"He…" But I find I can't say it. "The Colonel, he…"

"…shot Tod," says Beatty.

"Oh!" Polly claps her hand over her mouth. She sits down then stands up and begins to undress Beatty. "Oh, my little love, you're all skin and bone. I don't believe what you've told me..." She rubs away tears with the back of her hand and forces a smile. "But we're all safe now, and, oh, my little cherub..." But she can't finish the sentence.

I stand, not sure where to go next. The Colonel will be looking for us — but he might not think I'm daft enough to run here. Whatever happens I need to keep Beatty hidden and Polly safe. I can't lose them too.

"Quick, get new clothes on her, and both of you, let's get upstairs and see Ma, then I want to get you into hiding."

"Do you think we're next?" Polly asks, rubbing at Beatty's wet hair and peeling off her thin muslin gown.

"He won't stop at anything." I think for a moment. "We'll go to the Katz house. Mary'll hide you, even Mr K might hide you, but first, let's see Ma."

"I want to see Ma, I want her to hug me," says Beatty, holding out her arms for Polly to dry. "Is Mr Katz the man with the funny nose?"

"Yes," says Polly. "But it's a very nice nose — just rather large."

"He came to the river shed."

"What?"

"Yes — he came and I think it was him that put me in the bag."

"What?" I say.

"You think nice Mr Katz did it?" asks Polly. "That makes no sense, does it, Athan?"

"Beatty," I say, crouching down. "Yesterday. Did anyone take you to Mr Katz's house in a carriage?"

"What do you mean, Athan?" asks Beatty. "I haven't been anywhere. I've been in the river shed the whole time."

I sit back against the stove. It's almost completely cold but I'm so freezing it warms my back. "Beatty never went anywhere. She never needed to. And I gave him the plans. No wonder he looked so pleased at being the go-between."

"So where do we go then, Athan? Where can we hide?" asks Polly.

"Here," I say. "In this house. It's the safest place. If Ma realises, she'll guard you with her life. Come on, let's show her."

Polly wraps Beatty in a piece of heavy wool cloth and I bundle her up the stairs. Polly goes first and, looking back towards me to show that it's safe, we carry her into the room.

"Oh!" Ma screams. "OH!" She looks as if she'll collapse, but she grips the back of the chair and gapes at us.

"What ever?" Mrs Love half stands, her mouth falling open. "What on earth…?"

"Child!" Ma stammers, staggering towards us. "Oh, child…"

"Mamma, Mamma!" Beatty calls, and reaches her arms out to Ma, who wrenches her from us and squeezes her tight. Beatty's muddy hair sticks to Ma's cheek. Ma's tears wash it off. Polly put her arms around them both, a huge grin stretching her face.

Grandma stays in her armchair and shakes her head. Then stuffs another piece of toast in her dribbling mouth.

"Well," says Mrs Love. "Well, I never."

I pour her another cup of tea. She looks more shocked than Ma.

"Where were you, child?" asks Ma between kisses.

"With a vexatious woman," says Beatty. "She wasn't nice, but she gave me lots of paper for my birds, and fed me chocolate."

"Who was she?" Ma looks muddled. "What on earth would she want with you?"

"It was Colonel Blade, with her," says Beatty, kissing Ma back.

Ma's face is a picture of confusion. She glances at me.

"He had me stolen. He asked me questions all about Athan. And Mr Chen, and poor Tod, and even Columbine, but I didn't say nothing." Beatty grins. "Nothing at all. And Athan and Tod, they rescued me, but he shot Tod – right through his heart – and he drowned."

"What, child? I don't understand," says Ma. "What's this about Tod? And do you mean, that Athan was right?" She turns towards me, her arms open wide. "Tell me, tell me it—"

The door crashes open and the Colonel thunders into the room. His blue eyes flash wildly and little specks of foamy spit fleck his whiskers. His jacket's got sweat under the armpits and his waistcoat's hanging unbuttoned.

In one hand he's holding one of Beatty's birds. In the other, a pistol.

He glares at every one of us.

"You!" he shouts, pointing at me with the pistol. "You rat…"

I keep my back to the wall, waiting for the shot. I glance at Polly. She grabs Beatty and slips behind the day bed, helping herself to a warming pan as she goes. Ma stands stock-still in the middle of the room.

"I knew I knew you from somewhere." She takes a step towards him. "You were Columbine's fancy man, weren't you?"

He ignores her and makes as if to grab me, but I'm quick and over a chair before he gets near. He levels his pistol, catches Ma's eye, but keeps it trained on me.

"You ruined her years ago – and you'd move on and ruin me, would you?" She takes another step towards him. On her way she grabs the poker from the fireside. "Why, you evil man, you wicked creature," she hisses. The poker swings loosely from her hand. Her eyes flash. "You've used me, you've used poor mad Columbine." She takes another step towards him. "You've stolen my daughter and set me against my son."

"And murdered Tod!" shouts Beatty.

"Did I get 'im? Good!" says the Colonel. "Less vermin in this town."

"You monster – you barbarian – you bloodsucker!" Ma stamps her foot closer to the Colonel.

"Don't come closer, woman. I'll shoot your son quick as I'll shoot his friend. I'd be within the law, it'd be self defence."

"Self defence? I'll give you something to defend yourself from." Ma's poker whacks into his shoulder.

"Ouch!" he shouts, stepping back.

"You godless thing," she mutters, swinging the poker again. "That boy Tod was an angel."

"He was gutter food."

"Gutter food! At least he'd an ounce of guts! You – you, sneaking about, stealing our hearts and our children – you're as low as mud!"

"Ha!" He grabs at the poker but Ma's fast and she whisks it away. He takes a step towards her but she doesn't flinch. "You're no better yourself. You're a hideous trollop from a hideous city." He waves his gun about. Grandma hides her head behind the wing of the armchair.

Ma doesn't seem to notice even though she must know he'd shoot, never mind that we're all watching. They circle each other in the middle of the room, like bare-knuckle fighters. "You used me – you stole my children," she speaks quietly. "You took advantage of a lonely woman and a child." She takes up all the space. She's magnificent.

The Colonel spits on the floor. He doesn't answer her.

Everyone holds their breath.

Beatty and Polly crouch on the floor behind the day bed. I inch towards the door. The Colonel's eyes are fixed on Ma and the poker.

Ma stares at the pistol.

Ma makes her move. Hoisting the poker high behind her head, she swipes it down on the Colonel's hand so that the pistol flies high in the air and discharges so loudly the room appears to shake. A hole appears in the plaster by the fireplace.

"Beast!" shouts Ma, striking him again. "Beast!"

"Oh shut up, woman!" He steps forward to grab the poker from her, but Ma's too strong. Her huge arms push against him and she kicks his shins.

"You made a fool of me!" she shouts.

A chair tips, and silk and threads spew across the floor.

I beckon to Polly and she pushes Beatty ahead of her round the back of the room, still hidden by cushions. The gun's lying by the fireplace, right next to the fight. Horrible.

The Colonel rests his foot on the pistol. "Don't throw words at me, woman. I—"

She brings her knee up to his groin. I lunge for the gun but he kicks down on my thumb. "Aargh! You fat cow!"

"S'teeth!" I mutter. I try again, but he won't let it go, even with Ma struggling and kicking. The room's all legs and arms and thumping, pictures sliding from the walls, a table overturns, but the gun's still lying there on the rug.

Polly and Beatty are out of the door now, crashing down the stairs.

"Poll! Store cupboard. And…"

Polly stops, looking back up at me. "Athan?"

"No matter what happens next, I'll be back for you – I promise."

"How long this time, Athan?" Beatty calls. But I can't answer because the Colonel's back crashes into me, knocking the air from my lungs.

"Think me a mere woman! Oooh!" Ma lunges forward and sinks her teeth into his nose.

"Well done, Molly!" Mrs Love claps her hands and picking up the fire tongs smacks the Colonel on the back with them.

"Ow!" he screams. I make another lunge for the gun, but his boot's quicker than my hand.

I'll have to abandon it. It's more important to get him out of the house and away from everyone. It's me he wants; me and the machine. I wait on the landing although I'd love to run away, listening to the crashes as Ma flings vases and furniture across the room and the whole floor shakes.

"Can't fight off a mere woman!" I shout into the room.

There's a second's silence.

"Athan, careful!" calls Ma.

But the Colonel's boots thump on the floor; he's coming towards the door. "I'll get you, lad! No little starvelin' thief gets the better of Mordecai Blade."

I wait until I can hear his feet on the landing, then race down the stairs into the empty shop. Something crashes upstairs and I hear Ma bellow once more, then Mrs Love screams and the Colonel's boots thunder down the staircase. I wait on the pavement. I want to run, but he needs to see me, although I'm going to have to be fast. Faster than I've ever been.

A little way down the hill the road curves away to the river. I trot on down, within sight of the shop but giving myself some distance. All the time, I gulp more air than I need. I stretch my legs, swing my arms, ready for the race. The door of the shop clangs, and he swears behind me.

"Boy!" he shouts.

I run flat out.

Chapter 29

I run as fast as my legs can move, racing down the last piece of the hill and round to the left, the river on my right, and for a little while the gap widens. I'm swinging round past a timber warehouse when a cart unloading wood blocks the road, and I waste time working out which way to dodge. When I turn back, he's gaining on me. He's jangling and swearing and thumping and sweating, and obviously out of breath, but he's fast, with longer legs and more fury.

Veering left into the warren of the main town, I skip through the market stands and the handcarts. I know this piece like the inside of my own head.

I know that the pavement past the fishmonger's will be slippy, and that the piles of cabbage leaves are deeper than they look. If I can get him to lose time on those, then I'll be far enough ahead and can hide somewhere.

I jump over the fishmonger cobbles and listen for the roar of fury as he skids, but it doesn't come because he doesn't run that way. Instead he races across in front of me heading me back towards the warehouses and the empty parts of town.

I need to breathe.

I need to stop.

"Thief!" he shouts. "Stop the beggar!" And the people I pass turn to grab at my clothes.

My legs are pounding the pavement, screaming at me to stop, but I manage to pick up speed and charge back up through the abbey courtyard, whirling the red-faced people fresh out of the baths, tripping on the sedan chairmen and blundering on to the alley ways at the bottom of town.

"Hey, Athan!" someone shouts, but I run on, trying to lose Blade in the mess of tiny houses and workshops near Southgate.

"How'd you make it work, little scumbag? How's that machine made?" Suddenly close, the Colonel's shout booms down the narrow lanes. I halt by the downpipe from the roof of a large warehouse, buried in a tiny alley of washing lines and barrels. My legs are exhausted but my arms are strong, and I haul myself up like I've done so many times before, until my fingers reach into the leaf-filled gutter and I can heave myself on to the tiles. It's a long way up, and I stop to catch my breath. I listen; something's clanging down there.

Oh God, he's climbing the gutter.

But I've still got an advantage up here. Surely he can't be used to running over the rooftops. I skitter over the tiles, away from him. "You've cut your own throat now, lad." He scrambles on to the edge of the roof behind me. We're maybe fifty yards apart, and it's only a small jump up to the next building, a taller squarer warehouse with a flat roof.

I take a moment to breathe, put my hands on my knees to get the air to my lungs but I don't take my eyes off him. He does the same.

His face is purple, sweating.

"I can get you, lad. Easy."

I'm not going to waste my breath speaking.

"I can make you rich, boy. Why won't you let me?"

I still keep quiet. I'm watching his hand creeping slowly down his side to the pistol, which is sticking out of the top of his boot.

"You can shoot me," I pant. "But then you'll never

be able to build it."

"They looked at the plans, lad, but they were all rubbish." His eyes meet mine. "But you knew that, didn't you?" He's drawing the pistol out of his boot and, without looking, he loads it with lead and charges, like a man who's been trained to fight in the dark.

"They're not — but I don't think you're going to believe me." I take a step back until I'm teetering on the edge of the roof. Between my ankles I can see the gap and then the next roof.

"You've been clever and foolish all in one, lad. Clever t'get thy sister back, but silly — very silly — to think I wouldn't come after you." He moves a pace towards me. "And stupid to think you're t'only one 'as played on the rooftops. You won't get away, you know."

He smiles and reaches one hand towards me, the other steadying the gun so that it points at my head.

So I jump. It's backwards and I twist in the air and, by luck, land on the roof above, my legs already running. Without looking back I leap straight from the flat roof to a shorter building, loosely tiled and trembling under my feet, so I have to run along the ridge in case the whole thing collapses.

At the end, I swing a glance backwards. The Colonel stands stock-still on the flat roof, the pistol balanced across his arm, the barrel pointing right at me.

God's teeth!

I throw myself flat.

CRACK! A shot bounces on the roof and skitters down the tiles.

I crawl forward.

He reloads.

CRACK! Another zings past my ear.

"Ready to give in yet, lad? Call it a day?"

Below the edge of the roof is a long drop but there's a stack of barrels leaning up against the wall opposite. I might make it. I might break my ankle; then again, better than being shot.

CRACK! This time the bullet burns through my coat and nicks my elbow, stinging like a viper. Pain races down to my hand and back. It's hit my funny bone.

Not funny at all.

I swing my legs round and drop on to the ground, my ankle giving way as I fall and plunging me sideways into the wall so that I have to run awkwardly, dodging through an open courtyard, expecting another shot.

It comes a second later. Blade's there too, behind me in the courtyard, his pistol smoking; he misses and chips of stone fly past my ear from the wall. I race off. At least this way he has to stop each time he wants to reload. If he wants to keep on trying to shoot me,

I might actually get ahead of him.

If he doesn't kill me first.

I pick up a plank and scuttle along the alley with it on my back like a turtle. It might stop a bullet.

"Lad!" he calls. "Athan!"

I crouch behind a water tank. My plank now protecting my feet, listening to his voice, which sounds a way off and out of breath.

"See reason, lad. You'll not get away. I've a gun and you haven't."

I open my mouth to reply, but stop myself just in time, realising that he probably doesn't know where I am. It's dim here, dank and dotted with rubbish; he won't be able to see me. I need to stay silent and hidden.

It doesn't take long for my leg to go dead. I have to cram my knuckles in my mouth as the blood makes it back through to my foot. I try standing and upset a sheet of metal leaning against a wall. It crashes to the cobbles, echoing around the walls.

"S'teeth," I hear the Colonel muttering close by.

My legs start running again before I've even asked them to, and I reach the riverside and the rotten jetties just as another ball whizzes past my knees. His firing's wild and I hope it stays that way as the river now cuts me off and there's almost nowhere left to hide.

A stack of planks on the side give me an idea. I tip them into the water, pushing them out into the stream. In the gloomy light it does look a little like someone swimming. I duck back towards the wooden posts that stick out from the bank and pick my way over them, water sloshing over my boots.

I can't hear him any more, and waste a second turning to look.

He's standing staring at the planks, he raises his pistol and lets off a shot.

CRACK!

He watches the planks float on down the river, tilting his head from side to side as if checking for signs of life.

The mossy wood under my feet is soft and slippery but I keep going on towards Tod's place, not looking back and hoping that Blade will stay and shoot at the wood again, but a moment later:

CRACK!

This time it's the rotting planks beneath me that jump with the bullet.

"If you won't play along, then I'll have to kill ye!" he shouts.

There's no choice but to keep going along the rotten wooden pathway, so I run, my feet slithering and sliding, lurching from side to side as the Colonel's bullets ring out around my head.

CRACK!

CRACK!

He's getting faster at loading and firing.

CRACK!

Fifty paces to Tod's place. I can see the roof and what looks like the kite, standing free on the little platform outside. Someone's up there.

"Hey!" I yell.

The figure turns. It's Mary; she waves.

"He's behind me!" I shout.

As if to prove my point, the Colonel lets fly.

CRACK!

"Ye little brat, I'll 'ave ye. You'll be nothing better than dog's meat by the time I've done with ye!"

The side of the wood yard looms up. Two of the planks are loose and I slide through the gap just as another shot lodges in the wood by my ear.

Dammit, he's getting better.

"I'll mince ye, string y'up by your guts, like the old man — an' you'll squeal, lad, like a stuck pig. He did." His voice is getting closer, louder. "I can keep y'alive, kicking and screaming with y'r bits 'anging out, or feed you y'r own little fingers like that auctioneer. And y'r precious little sister, she can weep by your grave. If I don't mince her too. And I'll marry your other sister."

I push through the gap into the coffin yard where Mr Ballon the undertaker's doing something horrible with a jug and a bucket of offal on a brazier.

He looks startled at the noise, especially when he hears the Colonel's voice ringing through from outside. Really close this time. "Then we'll be related – thee and me," shouts the Colonel. "Shame y'won't be there to see us wed!"

"If you can't help, get out the way!" I shout to Mr Ballon. He steps aside and I charge past, catching the brazier with my jacket. It falls and rolls across the floor, live coals scattering into the sawdust, but I don't stop. Mr Ballon shouts behind me and I race up the ladder to get across the workshop to Tod's loft. Behind me clamour breaks out. The Colonel must have made his way in. I didn't think Mr Ballon would stop him, but he might hold him up.

The ladder takes too long to climb, my legs are slow, but another shot from the Colonel keeps me moving, this time grasping for a weapon, anything at all. I arm myself with a broom handle, it's useless against the gun but it makes me feel stronger.

The hatch into Tod's loft feels smaller than ever and when I burst out the other side the space is unrecognisable. Three walls remain but the fourth has gone. Even though the roof's still partly there, it's freezing and wet, but Mary stands caught in the wind, wild and wet and angry. Raw-faced, she's pouring liquid into the brass engine. The kite's all stretched out and it looks poised, ready.

"Athan," she says, turning towards me. "I've done it — it's all ready to go — I've finished what you started." Her hands are black and chunks of her hem are missing, as if she's torn them off for rags.

"Mary?" I say.

"When I heard he was dead — I came down. I finished it, I've linked it all up."

"How?"

She smiles a sad smile. "I saw the plans. I knew how it went together. I couldn't bear..."

She grabs the hem of her dress and uses it to blow her nose. "So I don't want to waste it. It's got to fly, it's got to escape, take it away — give it to the right people. You've got to go with it, for me, for Beatty, for Mr Chen, for Tod."

"Where shall I take it?" I say.

"West or go south. Africa." Her eyes are bright, almost mad.

"You devious little worm! When I catch up with you you'll wish you'd never been born." The Colonel shouts from under our feet and lets off the pistol so that a chunk of floor board leaps into the air.

"Hurry up, Athan," says Mary.

CRACK!

"No," I say. "We'll go together. We'll get out of this building, out of this town, safe, and then we'll win the prize. You and me. For Tod. For Mr Chen."

A woman's voice joins the clamour below us.

"Me and you?" says Mary, wiping her oily hands on her skirt.

"Yes. Come on! This thing'll never fly if we're dead."

Like someone in a dream, Mary stoops and wedges herself under the kite, her skirt billowing over the side. "Just pull that back," she mutters, pointing to the rear of the kite, which is entangled with a length of stretchy stuff.

A catapult.

Tod made a catapult.

"It's time, Mary. Let's get out of here." A waft of woodsmoke drifts up to me. I feel calm, my breathing slow and measured as if I know what I'm doing, as if I've always known, and as if I know why.

"Use your legs to push backwards. I'll hold on to the back until we're ready," I say.

The woman's voice gets louder. It isn't Ma or Polly – or the sharp-faced woman. "Call the boy a deceiver? That's fat, coming from you! You'd play cards with

Lucifer himself and win."

More shouting comes from below, and with it more smoke. The voices are muddled.

I pull back on the catapult. There are thumps and crashes and the whole building shakes.

Bang!

But this time it isn't a bullet. Instead, the little engine with the fan bursts into life and sparks fly until it settles into a sound like the hum of a million bees. We shoot forward across the tiny runway of the loft, and my feet leave the ground and the edge of the roof comes up faster than I can understand.

My legs hang loose in the air and the kite swings down through the drizzle towards the river. Mary pushes the bar and the kite twists upwards, somehow grabbing at the air and climbing. We turn — how, I don't know — and brush the side of the building. The kite judders and sways then rises again to skim over the tiles of the house next door.

My stomach has stayed on the roof; my body is miles above. It's like nothing I've ever felt before and it's wonderful.

For a second the kite stops, hovering, still as a hawk above the wood yard.

I watch the flames catch in the yard below and Tod's uncle lugging out coffins. Some of them filled.

Beside me Mary's laughing, her hair floating madly around her face and shoulders, her skirt dotted with roses of blood – hers or mine, I don't know.

A shot rings out, louder than the bees.

The Colonel is there on the roof, his pistol smoking. He points his gun at us. Another puff of smoke and something whizzes through the air, popping against the silk above my head. Underneath the Colonel's boots the fire is roaring through the building. From up here in the sky he looks like some mad devil standing over the flames of hell. The back wall of the loft's almost gone; there's almost nothing left.

Another wild shot whistles though the cloth. I need more height, or more distance, but I can't control it. Winds catch us and throw the kite towards the building again, laughing and coughing we rise up on the heat, higher and higher.

Glancing down, I see the Colonel's smile. He lifts the pistol again and this time we're so close a child could hit us. He aims; he's got all the time in the world. Smoke's pouring from what's left of the walls of the loft but he doesn't move, just stretches his mouth into a wide grin.

I close my eyes, I'm in the sky but...

"Aaaaargh!" From the smoke, a woman in green appears. She teeters on the tiny unburned space. It's

Columbine, madder than ever, her dress hanging from her shoulders, blackened and burned. Her crazy red hair singed and thin, her eyes blazing.

She catches his arm as he fires, tilting the gun so that the bullet passes through the silk above Mary's head. I look down and Columbine shouts up to me, but her words are lost in the crackle of the flames.

Breathless, covered in the hot thick woodsmoke, we climb higher and higher, carried up by the intense heat while below they struggle, their bodies almost consumed by the blaze, flames bursting through the wood beneath their feet.

He swings his pistol to fire on her and she grabs him, her arms gripped so close around his jacket that he can't move; and then with a strength I didn't know she had, she takes him through the wall of the loft and into the fire below.

I see them fall together. The fire crawls up her dress and the orange flowers of flame bloom around her, lighting up her hair in a golden coronet.

And though his arms hold hers, clutching her in a strange embrace, his chill blue eyes turn towards me and lock on to mine until he vanishes.

We buried Tod. All of us, together. Mary and Polly made him a shroud sewn from the finest muslin and stitched with blue forget-me-nots.

Beatty sat on the coffin cart and held the flowers.

Ma led the mourners.

Grandma muttered incantations.

They would have buried Columbine too, but they couldn't find her body in the fire.

So we wrapped green ribbons around lilies and laid them with Tod in the cemetery in Widcombe.

We came home and ate seedcake and lemon posset and I went up to my room and cried.

Before the wake was over Mr Katz left town.

In a hurry.

He left his violin and Mary brought it round as a gift for Uncle.

So it was the end of February before Mary and I found how to win the prize. Polly read all the newspapers and wrote a letter for us, inviting the Duke of Roseberry to witness our flight.

On a fresh spring day, when the snowdrops were peeking out, we took the kite to the top of Landsdown. Tod's da and uncle carried it for us on the hearse, with two black horses pulling.

Ma handed out cheese and apples.

Two men in fine coats arrived and measured a furlong on the ground. They carried binoculars and had servants.

"Two attempts," they said. "You have two attempts."

They yawned and looked bored as we made our preparations. They obviously didn't think we were going to win.

It made Mary very serious. Very determined. She kept on checking everything: the stitches, the struts, the angle of the fan.

Polly mended the bullet holes with patches of green silk so that by the time the kite was ready it looked even more like a moth.

They all stood at the edge of the graveyard to watch.

"Go, Athan," said Mary, holding the wires of the electric box, her face streaked with oil and tears. "Good luck."

But I knew I didn't need the luck. I knew it would fly. I always knew it would fly.

So as I dreamed, the engine buzzed, the grass whizzed under my feet, and I flew, over the marker, over the cemetery, over the hearse, higher than I had ever been.

Than anyone had ever been.

Slowly I rose to float over the city and its builders. The golden blocks of stone laid out for the hungry stonemasons, the slates for the roofers. The great squares and circles stretched into the countryside, all roads leading to the city.

Above me the heavens. Above me space and freedom and glory.

But below me, everything I loved.